Prince of Sins and Shadows

FAE OF REWYTH BOOK 2

EMILY BLACKWOOD

xoxo Emily

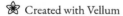

CHAPTER 1
Jade

Hunger had never been a stranger.

When I was ten years old, my kid sister Tessa and I had wandered our boney, exhausted bodies to the nearest market in town to steal food. It had been days since we had eaten anything but bread crumbs, and our father was nowhere to be found.

Tessa was still a child. We both were, really. But one of us had to grow up if we were going to survive.

It wasn't unusual for us to go hungry. It wasn't unusual for any humans to be on the verge of starving. It still wasn't. But we had never suffered that long before.

We dragged ourselves the multiple miles to the market and smiled kindly at everyone we passed.

Our feet bled from the rough road and the summer sun scorched our skin. Tessa nearly fainted more than once, and I remember thinking she wasn't going to make it. But she did. She was always stronger than I gave her credit for, even back then.

When we got there, though, we were told to leave. *We can't help you*, the older man had said. *Come back with your parents or come back with some money.*

They didn't know we didn't have money. They didn't know we didn't have a parent worth mentioning. They took one look at us and guessed.

It was an accurate guess.

Tessa didn't cry, but I knew the hunger hurt her. It hurt me, too.

It wasn't the usual dull ache from lack of a solid meal. It was a special pain that only came with extreme emptiness. It was a pain that gave us little reason to keep going. Little hope. After a couple of days, though, you don't notice the pain. You don't notice the lack of hope. If you have any chance of surviving, you *can't* notice those things.

On our way home that day, during the endless hours that I spent thinking about every possible way to feed myself and my sister, we came across a small deer.

The deer was alone, just standing in a field of tall grass, out in the open. Up until then, I had seen only a handful of deer in my lifetime, and never that close to me. Never that calm. She was gorgeous, I remembered thinking that. And she stared at us, chewing on her food, like we were her friends.

She trusted us. She knew we would not hurt her.

But Saints, we were *so hungry.*

And I remembered how to hunt. My father had

dragged me with him a handful of times by that point, before he had started drinking again.

"Do it," Tessa had whispered, tugging on my hand. Her eyes were big and desperate, likely mirrors of mine. I was surprised that she would even suggest it, she was always one to love animals.

Tessa had stayed put as I approached the deer, just close enough so I could throw the knife I had taken from our father's things. I remembered how fast my heart was beating. This was our last chance, I thought.

It was this, or starving to death.

Tessa dropped to her knees in relief when my blade sliced the animal's skin, sinking deep into its flesh.

I nearly did, too. It was the one and only time I had ever managed to kill a deer that way.

We did not cry as the animal's blood covered our hands. We did not cry as we dragged it the last mile to our cottage. We did not cry as we worked together to slice it apart, piece by piece, and roast the delicate meat over our fire.

We did not cry.

It wasn't until Tessa was deep asleep, and I had scrubbed our hands dry of any blood and any small memory of the beautiful creature, that I let myself grieve.

Not for the deer, although I felt bad about what I had to do.

No, I grieved for myself. Because a part of me died that day, too.

I had pushed the memory away for so long. I didn't

want to remember all the horrid things I had done to survive. It was easy to forget those things when I was living in Rewyth.

When I was living in *luxury*.

But in the two days I had been in Fearford, living with the humans like mere scum on the bottom of the fae's shoe again, I remembered every last detail.

We were so exhausted by the time we made it to Fearford that I didn't care to even glance around. I ate the poor excuse of a dinner served to me and I happily let someone lead me to an open structure where I had nearly passed out on a cot next to dozens of other girls. Even if Malachi argued about it the entire time.

He had nothing to worry about here. We were humans, after all.

But now, after who knows how many hours of laying in the corner, I was curious to see where exactly we ended up.

"Good," a voice said as soon as I began sitting up. "You're up. We have a lot to cover today, and your nap time is about over, so let's get going."

"Excuse me?" I asked. My voice was groggy and I had to squint through the morning sunlight to see the dark-haired woman sitting on the cot next to me, clearly waiting on me to wake up. How long had she been there?

Where was Malachi?

She rolled her eyes, as if my confusion was somehow an inconvenience.

"You've been sleeping for days, and we have some questions about you and your friends. Let's go. He doesn't like to wait."

I massaged my temples with my fingertips and squeezed my eyes shut. "Who's 'he'?"

"The boss man around here. He was kind enough to let you sleep it off, but if I were you—" she leaned closer to me and glanced around us before finishing, "—I would get your ass moving, sunshine."

She stood up and headed for the door. My body resisted every movement as I pulled myself to my feet. The cracked skin on my back was healing, but every ounce of my body still ached. I didn't even want to know if I looked as wounded as I felt.

Step by step, I walked past dozens of cots filled with girls who stared curiously at me. I ignored the murmurs and whispers as I followed the dark-haired girl out of the building and into the blinding sunlight.

I knew Fearford would be poor. I knew it would be dirty and the people would be hungry. I wasn't expecting anything more than a shithole of poverty.

This was a city of humans, after all.

On the way here, Malachi's sister, Adeline, had filled me in on most of the politics I needed to know. She told me that all the humans used to live together in poverty, and that Fearford had separated themselves in hopes of coming out on top. They were flanked by two of the biggest fae kingdoms, Rewyth and Trithen.

How these humans thought that would benefit

them was beyond me. It's not like the fae were just going to give their goods and resources to humans.

But here, on the complete opposite side of Rewyth, was Fearford. A large shithole of hunger, poverty, and powerlessness.

"I'm Sadie, by the way," she said. "You're Jade, right?"

I looked at her again. She seemed to be about my age. Her shoulder-length, dark hair had small braids throughout, and her shirt exposed her long, toned arms. She looked like a fighter. A survivor.

Anyone who lived here would have to be.

"That's right," I sighed.

We walked past numerous shacks that looked as if they would tumble down any second. Only a few other humans nodded acknowledgements at us, but for the most part, they kept their heads down.

Fearford was bigger than I expected, I had to give it that much. Rows and rows of tents and makeshift housing spanned as far as I could see.

It reminded me of home, it truly did. Only Tessa wasn't here. My father wasn't here. As if either of them would come to see me, anyway.

Was it even possible to get back home?

"Where is everyone else?" I asked.

"The fae, you mean?" Sadie asked. I couldn't decipher any emotion in her voice. "They're still here, don't worry. Your big bad army of freaks wouldn't leave without you."

I let out a breath. I don't know why it surprised me that they stayed. The fae hated humans so much, why would they accept help from them?

But part of me also knew Malachi wasn't going anywhere if I was here. And after finding his own mother with me in the forest...

We had a lot to discuss.

Sadie caught me staring at the makeshift homes around us and stopped walking. "Not as glamorous as the fae castle, I imagine," she said.

I shook my head. "Maybe not," I said. "But at least everyone here doesn't want me dead."

Sadie took a deep breath and kept walking. "I wouldn't be too sure about that," she mumbled.

"What? I'm awake here for a few minutes and people already hate me?"

She slowed down so I could catch up to her pace. "It's not that people hate you specifically," she said. "But the fae aren't welcome here. If it wasn't for your prince's mother, you all would have never stepped foot inside of Fearford. She's the one that convinced us it would be okay. Without her, you would be out of luck."

I held back a laugh. If the fae wanted to enter Fearford, these humans couldn't stop them. Her confidence was inspiring, though.

"Mal's mother...how long has she lived here? Why does she want us here so badly?"

Sadie glanced at me and rolled her eyes. "You have a

lot to learn, Jade. Maybe save those questions for her. I'm sure she'd just *love* to talk to you about it."

"But what does that have to do with me? I'm human, not fae. Nobody should have a problem with me being here."

"You're kidding, right?"

I waited for her to continue.

"You're married to the Prince. How do you think that makes you look, Jade? You might be human, but to everyone else here, you're one of them."

I didn't expect to feel embarrassed, but I did.

Yes, I was married to Malachi. But it wasn't because I wanted to be. I had no choice but to marry Malachi.

How much did they know about all of that? Had Malachi told them everything? Had his mother?

I decided not to argue, and stayed silent as Sadie led us to the others through the small city of Fearford. By the time we got there, even though it was just a few minutes of walking through tents and wooden structures, sweat was beading off my forehead and dripping down my neck.

I followed her through a thick steel door into what looked like the only substantial building in Fearford. I was immediately greeted by thick, stale air and the smell of more sweat.

Great.

"Welcome, Jade," a sugary, young man's voice chirped. "We've been waiting for you to awaken. I trust you slept well, then?"

My eyes adjusted to the dim lighting of the room. Dark steel constructed four thick walls, enclosing the space with barely enough light to see. A makeshift desk stood in the middle of the room, and the thin, sun-kissed man who greeted me sat behind it.

"Well enough," I responded. He looked younger than I expected, just like Sadie. Definitely too young to be the sole leader of Fearford. "Where's everyone else?" I asked. *Where was Malachi?*

"They'll be here," he replied. He closed some sort of book he was holding and stood slowly from the desk. "We've heard quite a lot about you, Jade Weyland."

"It's Jade Farrow," I corrected. I might be married in the eyes of the fae, but I was still Jade Farrow. "Not Weyland."

"Really?" he questioned. "Does your *husband* know that?"

My stomach dropped. I fought to keep still. "Maybe you should ask him that question..."

"Isaiah," he finished.

"*Isaiah*," I repeated.

"I can't say he's been entirely forthcoming with information since your arrival," Isaiah continued, walking around the desk. "None of them have, despite Esther's best efforts."

"Esther?" I questioned.

"Malachi's mother," he answered.

I crossed my arms over my chest and smiled. My instincts told me not to show him weakness. Not to show him confusion. I ignored that bomb and continued, "Our people hate each other. Fearford is a dump compared to Rewyth, and I'm sure my friends are expecting you to kick them out at any minute. So yeah, I bet they've been *real* forthcoming. Where is *Esther*, anyway? What's going on?"

Isaiah's eyes dragged down my body as he stood there, leaned against his desk, with a smug look on his face. If it weren't for the exhaustion I felt, I might've slapped the look off him myself. But I let it slide this one time.

Malachi was going to *hate* this guy.

"They've been staying in a separate location. The other citizens haven't been too happy about our guests. I'm sure you understand. It was a bit of a surprise, after all. We don't have many guests here. Especially not fae."

"You had to have known we were coming," I said.

Surprise flashed across his face before he quickly covered it. "What makes you think that?"

"The King didn't tell you? He sent us here," I chose each word carefully.

Isaiah laughed. "The King of Rewyth hasn't spoken to us in years. We have no contact with your people, darling."

My people? Darling? Who the Saints did this guy think he was? I took a deep, calming breath. My mind raced through all the possible things to say to him when the door swung open again.

"She's not your darling," Malachi's voice boomed as he waltzed into the room. It only took him two strides to cross the room and stand next to me, so close that his bare shoulder brushed against mine. He was in the same clothes he had been wearing on our journey here, only now, they were ripped and blood-stained. "And I suggest you watch the way you speak to my wife."

CHAPTER 2
Jade

M alachi's mother followed behind him, and the solid door shut behind them once more.

I pushed away the butterflies I felt by being so close to him again. I hated that he did this to me.

He was *fae*. I was *forced* to marry him.

Yet, here I was, absolutely obsessed by how close he was standing to me.

We had bigger things at stake here.

Malachi glanced at me, and I quickly looked away from his dark eyes and focused my attention on his wrists.

On the chained restraints that cuffed them.

"Chains?" I asked Isaiah. "Are you kidding me? You can't actually believe that those are doing anything."

"They do enough," Isaiah responded. His relaxed demeanor was gone. It had changed into a broad-chested, stiff one to match Malachi's presence. Very different than the boyish presence he had just moments ago. "It's more of a formality for the others, anyway. Malachi knows we're on the same team here."

As if he stood a chance.

I looked back at Malachi. "Those things really stop you? You can't break out?"

Malachi's gaze lingered on me, as if he were drinking up every feature. I couldn't look away. I was frozen.

Without saying a word, Malachi flexed his wrists, just once, and broke out of the small iron cuffs.

Even as they clattered to the floor, he didn't break our gaze.

Sadie snickered, and Malachi's mother mumbled some sort of warning.

I broke our stare first, turning my attention back to Isaiah and Sadie. "See?" I gestured. "What was the point of that? Are they supposed to be prisoners here?"

"Not prisoners," Malachi's mother, Esther, spoke up. "You all are our guests."

Malachi shifted on his feet next to me but didn't speak up. "Yet you put your own *son* in chains," I retorted.

Now that I knew this woman was Malachi's mother, I saw the resemblance. They had similar eyes, eyes that filled with power. On the journey to Fearford, I hadn't had the energy to ask the woman any questions.

Now, however, I felt particularly well-rested.

"I know I might have missed some things while I

was asleep," I continued, unable to keep the growing attitude out of my voice, "so why don't you go ahead and fill me in on what the Saints is going on?"

Malachi and Esther glanced at each other but didn't say anything.

It appeared that everyone knew more than they were letting on.

I wasn't in the mood.

"If anyone has some crazy shit to tell me, like what we're doing here and why Malachi was in chains, then I suggest you start talking."

"Yes," Malachi continued, focusing his attention on Isaiah. "Why don't you tell her why I'm in chains here."

"Don't be dramatic," Esther chimed in. "It's just a safety measure."

"And where have you been?" I asked her. "You show up in those woods with no warning and put a knife to my throat? You have Malachi's brothers nearly kill me? I think I deserve an explanation."

Her soft smile disappeared. Malachi took the smallest step toward me.

"Listen up, child," she started. "I don't owe you anything. Certainly not an explanation. I saved your life on multiple occasions, times when you didn't even know you were in trouble." She paused and examined my face. It took everything in me to stay silent. "You have a loud mouth for someone in the presence of the Prince of Shadows. Has she always been this way, son?"

Malachi rolled his shoulders back and clenched his

fists. I waited for him to yell, to lose his temper. But instead, he laughed, low and eerie.

When I built the courage to meet his face, he was already staring at me.

Malachi, the man who could never keep his mouth shut, was at a loss for words.

A lot more had changed since I had been sleeping than I thought.

"Are we done here?" I said to Isaiah. "Because my *husband* and I need to have a little chat."

"That's the thing, Jade," he responded. "I know you think the King of Rewyth sent you here, but it's not that simple." He glanced at Malachi, then back to me. "The humans won't like it. Not at all."

"Why?" I asked. "I'm human. I'm one of them."

Malachi's mom shook her head and mumbled under her breath.

"Not to them, you're not," he said, repeating Sadie's words from earlier. "They'll view you as a traitor."

"That doesn't make any sense. This union doesn't hurt them, it helps them. With Mal's connections we can bargain for food and other goods. That's the whole reason we came here!"

"Not the only reason," Mal's mom chimed in. "Which is what we need to talk about. All of us."

My heart sank to my stomach. I had a feeling something was waiting for us in Fearford. It was never going to be as simple as the King had let on.

"Did you know about this?" I asked Mal, keeping my voice low.

He took a deep breath. "They told me while you were asleep. We didn't want to wake you."

"Great," I mumbled back. "I missed all the fun, it seems."

"Fun is an interesting choice of words, but yes. We have a lot to talk about."

"Start talking then," I responded. Annoyance dripped from my voice.

"As you know," Mal started before shifting uncomfortably, "for decades now, I believed that my father was holding my mother hostage somewhere, in an unknown location, so that I would continue to cooperate. It was his way of keeping my power in check, because power like mine is incredibly rare and incredibly powerful. After talking to Esther here, I learned that that was not the case at all. Esther left Rewyth long ago, after she discovered how cruel my father could be."

"You just left? How is that even possible?"

"I have very powerful friends," she said. "And very powerful ancestors. It made things easier, and the King knew better than to come looking for me. Besides, it was embarrassing enough already. He had no problem moving on after I left, as you can tell by Malachi's siblings."

"You were working with Malachi's brothers? Why? And how?"

"It was difficult at first," she explained. "Finding ways to send messages back and forth was tricky, but it became easier over time. The boys eventually agreed to a blood oath, which made things much easier. Once I learned of the wedding, we made our plan to protect you. We *had* to protect you, Jade."

My mind was racing. "Hold on," I said, holding up my hands. "Everyone is just okay with this? Your mother tells you that her and your brothers have been conspiring behind your back, and you're okay with it?"

"They were saving your life, Jade."

"Why? Why me?"

Mal glanced at Esther, who stepped forward.

"Because I was told to."

"By who?"

Malachi stepped forward and grabbed my hand. "Jade," he whispered.

"No!" I blurted. "Stop treating me like I can't understand."

"Fine. Tell her," Malachi said, looking at Esther again. "She'll find out eventually."

A few painful seconds passed.

"You know I'm not fae," Mal's mother said. "But I'm not exactly human, either."

The words were a confirmation of what I already believed. I clenched my teeth and tried to control my breathing while she continued.

"I'm sure you've heard about witches that used to live with the fae. My bloodline is one of the eldest of the witches. One of the most powerful."

The shaking in my voice betrayed me as I asked, "You're a witch?"

"My bloodline has been going extinct for many reasons, but the lack of magic is one of the main reasons. Magic is like water, you see. Especially to us witches. It comes and goes, as natural as the wind. But a few decades ago, the magic us witches possessed began to retract. It became more and more difficult to use our power, until eventually it was entirely impossible without a sacrifice."

"So you used to have magic, but not anymore? How is that different from magic the fae possesses?"

"The fae are gifted, Jade. By the Saints or whomever you pray to. For whatever reason, the Saints have chosen them as worthy to carry their magic. We had a feeling this might be the case, though."

I waited for her to continue, ignoring the sick feeling growing in my gut. Esther stepped closer to me and lowered her voice.

"Our elder at the time told us of an ancient prophecy. She had said that a human would be the turning point for us, joining the fae magic with the magic of witches. That this human would return magic to its original form, back to the fae and the witches both to use freely without sacrifice."

Malachi stiffened next to me. He must not have known, either. "And what makes you think this human is me?"

The room seemed to be getting smaller, walls inching closer and closer to me with every passing second.

My mind was spinning. Esther didn't answer me,

she just continued to stare at me with those large, green eyes.

Pity. That's what I saw in her. She pitied me, no matter how hard she tried to hide it.

My heart was racing, and I suddenly became very aware of the sweat now dripping down my back.

"I think I'm going to be sick," I said. I didn't wait for anyone to respond to me. I shoved through the front door, past Sadie and Malachi's mother, and back into the blazing sunlight.

My stomach flipped over and over as I kept walking.

I took five more steps before I dropped to my knees and vomited.

Nothing made sense. I had lived my entire life in the human lands, and now I find out that I was somehow related to this witch's prophecy?

I vomited until my stomach was empty, and continued to heave with every breath.

The door slammed again in the distance. I knew it was Mal. I could feel his presence before he even said a word.

"Saints, Jade," he mumbled, rushing to my side and kneeling next to me. He placed a large hand on my back, a simple gesture that sent a shiver down my spine, even in the heat of day. "Are you alright?"

Tears and snot both dripped from my face. "No, definitely not. None of this is okay. None of this is normal."

"It's a lot to hear all at once," he said.

"Did you know?" I asked. "Did you know that I was different? That I was being protected?"

"No," he answered sternly. "I swear I didn't know. Did I think it was a miracle that you were still alive? Yes. Did I know my mother was behind it? No. And I definitely didn't know any of that crazy shit about the prophecy, or whatever my mother called it."

Tears dropped from my chin. Malachi studied my face for a moment, then caressed it with both of his hands, wiping my tears with his thumbs. "I'm still going to protect you, Jade. They might not like it, but you're still my wife."

A harsh laugh erupted from me. "I thought you were supposed to rule here. What happened to that plan?"

He sighed, cracking a smile himself. "Plans change, princess."

"And your mother?" I asked. Malachi just raised an eyebrow. "Aren't you supposed to be, like, traumatized or super pissed off or something? I mean, she left you. She's been gone all this time and you thought she was somewhere being tortured by your father."

He shook his head. "I can't even think about that right now. If I let myself get pissed, this entire city might burn."

"Wow," I replied. "Is it crazy that I've actually missed that temper of yours?"

"A little bit."

I smiled and let him press his forehead against mine.

"The humans might not respect our marriage, but we'll be out of here soon. We'll figure this out. And in the meantime, I'll protect you. Always." He said, his breath tickling my cheek.

"It might not be that simple," I said.

"I don't care. I don't care what I have to do. Shit, I don't care if I have to hide in a bunker until all of this is over. It'll end soon, and we'll get out of here."

"To go where? Rewyth?"

A smile spread across his face. "Anywhere we want."

"Fine," I whispered. "That better be a promise."

His hand still cradled my face, his thumb tracing my cheek lightly.

I wanted to kiss him. I wanted to do more than kiss him. I wanted to get out of here, away from his mother and all the other ridiculous people here in Fearford.

But Malachi was *fae*. He was dangerous, and here, he was trouble.

Isaiah had made that very clear.

Malachi inched closer, just a touch. Close enough for me to realize that his eyes, framed by black walls of thick lashes, had small specks of gold in them.

How hadn't I noticed that before?

The doors slammed open behind us again, and any tension that was lingering between us vanished.

I stood up before Malachi and put a few paces between us.

"There you are," Sadie chirped. I quickly wiped my face dry and turned to face her. "Look," she said. "There's a party tonight, it happens every full moon."

Her gaze shifted to Mal. "Come. Show the humans they can trust you. It might be worth a shot."

"That doesn't sound like a good idea," I said.

She raised her hands in a lazy shrug. "Do whatever you want, I honestly don't care. But it's not just you two in the picture. Your fae friends will have a hard time if the entire kingdom fears you two."

"Where are they? Serefin and Adeline?"

"They're fine," Mal said. "I'll take you to them. Follow me."

Sadie stepped forward and added, "I have to warn you, though. You might not like what you see. The humans and the fae have a strange relationship here in Fearford. You should brace yourselves."

"Brace ourselves for what? What do you mean?" I asked.

Sadie didn't answer. Just turned her back and walked away, her feet crunching on the ground with every step.

I glanced at Malachi, but he just shrugged his shoulders. He didn't know what she meant, either. And he didn't seem to care.

If one more person in this damned kingdom didn't answer my questions, I was really going to lose my mind.

Mal began walking away, mumbling something under his breath and leaving me to scramble behind him.

My mind was racing. Malachi hadn't really talked about what had been going on between us. We didn't have the time. He was my husband, after all. Didn't that answer any question I might have?

And Sadie had a good point. It wasn't just Malachi and I against the world. We had friends to take care of. And all of the humans hating us would not help.

Malachi's shoulders were wide. I imagined what his wings would look like if he dropped his glamour. It was Esther's idea to hide the fae wings. We were supposed to ease into the human lands, not march in with our wings out. Did it take energy to hold the glamour? Did it exhaust him to hide his fae features in the human lands?

I guess it didn't matter. Malachi was the enemy in the human lands, and while he could easily drop any rival who raised an arm against him, it would be a sign of war.

A war without his father's backing. A war with no army.

It wouldn't be humans against fae or fae against humans, it would be Malachi against the world.

And I would be forced to fight with him.

"Can you slow down?" I yelled from behind him. "Not all of us are seven feet tall with wings."

Malachi slowed enough for me to catch up, but didn't turn to face me.

"Hey!" I stomped forward and grabbed his arm, spinning him around to face me. He grabbed me by the arms, gripping tightly like he was still deciding what to do with me.

His eyes were wild and his chest rose and fell with shallow breaths.

"Don't walk away from me like that," I spat. He smiled amusingly, baring his teeth.

His eyes dropped to my lips and lingered there for a few seconds.

We hadn't talked about what we were doing with our *relationship*. There hadn't been time. Both of us were too busy trying to stay alive.

But with the entire human race despising our union, we had to figure it out. Soon.

His hands still gripped each of my arms. I was close to him. The closest I had been in a while. Did he feel the same way?

He tugged on my arms, causing me to slam into his chest.

"I'm not leaving you, Jade," he whispered close to my lips.

"Okay," was all I could manage to respond. "I don't plan on leaving you, either. I don't need to give the King of Rewyth any more reason to want me dead."

"Really?" He teased, a small smile on his lips. "Is that the only reason you don't want to leave me?"

His hands moved from my arms to my back, and I found myself placing my hands on his shoulders and around his neck.

I nodded once. "Yes," I breathed. "That's the only reason."

His hands moved to caress my side, dropping dangerously low.

"You swear?" he asked. A noise I didn't recognize escaped my mouth.

This time I couldn't bring myself to respond.

Malachi brought his mouth so close to mine that our lips touched, just barely, as we both breathed the same, electrified air.

"You're mine, princess," he spoke into my lips. "Whether you like it or not."

Malachi slammed his mouth into mine. The kiss wasn't gentle or exploring. It was rough and needy. He kissed me like I was the only thing keeping him alive, like I was his only hope at survival.

And I kissed him back.

My chest pumped adrenaline through my body as my hands splayed through Malachi's hair. I pressed my body against his as tightly as I could, not wanting a single inch of distance between us.

Malachi kissed me deeply, pulling me to him and dragging his hands across my body. His touch left a trail of fire, and I longed for him in ways I would never admit aloud.

Somewhere in our tangle of limbs and mouths, I realized what we were doing.

"Stop," I mumbled, pulling away enough to look at his face. What the Saints was I doing? "Stop, we can't do this. Someone will see us."

A devious look crossed his features. I knew that look. That was the look of someone who wanted to be caught. He wanted to cause trouble.

That was the look of the Prince of Shadows.

Malachi leaned in again, ready to continue where we left off, when Serefin shoved out of the door directly next to us and stepped into the sun.

"Someone already has," he announced.

I found myself scrambling away from Malachi and straightening my tunic that was now shoved up my back.

"There you are," Malachi said to Serefin. "We were looking for you."

"Really?" Serefin teased. "And where exactly did you think I was?"

Malachi glanced at me, clearly amused by my embarrassment.

"Would you like to answer that, Jade?" He smirked at me.

"No. I would not. Nice to see you again, Serefin. We have a lot to discuss."

"Indeed, we do, Lady Farrow."

I brushed past him and into the room he exited from.

My eyes adjusted to the darkness, and my jaw hit the floor.

CHAPTER 3
Malachi

"What's going on?" Jade asked. I had been dreading this moment. The moment Jade had to see how her *beloved* humans were treating the *monstrous* fae.

Part of me was curious to see her reaction. To see if she cared or not. To see if she would pity the fae or take the side of the humans.

The side. Is that what we were now? The enemy in these lands?

Adeline rushed forward and threw her arms around Jade. Jade staggered backward, but hugged her back.

"I'm so glad you're okay," Adeline whispered. I looked away, letting them have their moment as I surveyed the others.

My brothers.

If I could even call them that anymore. I had come so close to killing Lucien, so close to ending his useless life. I told him what would happen if anyone laid a finger on Jade. Lucien was chaotic and disobedient, he always had been.

Yet he was still alive.

I took a deep breath and reminded myself that none of that mattered now. With all the information my mother had given me and with the blood oath she made them take...

Nothing mattered now except that Jade was different. *Actually* different, and not just in the way I felt about her.

My mother seemed to think Jade was part of some sort of prophecy. Now that she was here and talking about it all, I remembered how my mother used to be. How crazy she had been about prophecies of all sorts. I didn't have many memories of my mother, but many of the ones I did have showcased her mania and obsession with these stories other villagers would tell her.

I even remembered being dragged by her into the villages when I was a child. She would listen to anyone who could tell her old stories about the mysterious girl who would either end their suffering once and for all or ruin the world with her failures.

Of course, I never listened to her. What would be considered suffering for us? We were fae royalty. But back then, my mother was just as respected as the eldest fae in Rewyth, if not more so because of her lineage.

Everyone bent a knee to her without hesitating. My father was different, though. People knelt before him because of fear. Not because of respect.

The entire kingdom grieved for years when she left.

My father and I were some of the only ones who knew she was still alive. Although I had to admit, I had my doubts over the decades.

If only I could trust her...

It's not that I *didn't* trust my mother, but something wasn't right. Why would she stay hidden all this time? The numerous wives I had that had been murdered by my father... she knew about them. She knew about them all and did nothing.

She stepped in to save Jade, and she let each of the others die at my father's hand.

Who cared about the prophecy? I had been tormented time and time again by my father, and the whole time I had looked for an assassin. An outside enemy.

And the whole time, it had been the King.

While I suffered for decades.

When I went to talk to her late last night, while Jade and the others were still asleep, she had little information to give me. *I tried to help them*, she had said. *I tried to help them but your father moved too quickly.*

Did I believe her? Saints, no. My mother had manipulated all of my four brothers to swear a blood oath to her. Adonis, Lucien, Fynn, and Eli. They wouldn't have done that willingly. A blood oath was serious, even to fae.

Esther was a powerful woman. If she wanted to save the lives of mere humans who were forced to marry me, she could have easily done it.

But no. Only Jade was spared. Only appearing after all these years.

"Good to see you again, brother," Adonis mumbled. Jade pulled away from Adeline and turned her attention to Adonis. To him and the chains that were loosely linked around his wrists and ankles.

"More chains?" She questioned. "Really?"

Adonis held his wrists up to show her. "Why just your brothers?" she asked me.

"Isaiah wanted to assure the humans that the *dangerous fae* were locked up."

She laughed. "And they let you stay out here?"

I caught myself smiling at Jade's bubbly laugh and I cleared my throat.

"It's more of an insurance policy. And I'm sure big bad Isaiah wants us to know who's in charge." I explained.

"But why?" She asked. Her big brown eyes looked at me. "Something's strange here. I can't tell exactly what, but something doesn't feel right."

I shook my head, quickly brushing off her words.

Mostly because they were true, but I didn't want her worrying about that. "It's fine." I said. "Nothing we can't handle. Once we get the annoying politics out of the way we might really like it here."

She looked around the room. "And you're all okay with this? With slumming it in Fearford while the fae live like royalty in Rewyth?"

It was my turn to laugh. I let my glamour drop, my wings flared out to my sides.

Jade's lips parted in surprise and her eyes drank up every inch. I couldn't deny that it thrilled me, knowing Jade *liked* how we looked as fae.

I would have never thought a human would like our flashy wings and pointed ears.

I rolled my shoulders back and said, "We are royalty, princess. I don't give a damn where we're at. Nobody tops us. Nobody."

She nodded slowly, but I swore I saw her lips curl slightly in the corners.

"Besides," I said. "This is just temporary."

"Oh yeah?" Lucien chimed in. "Because you think our father is just going to graciously change his mind? He'll kill her the second he gets his hands on her. You know that."

My fists clenched at the thought. Yeah, I did know that. Just like all my previous wives, my father wanted Jade dead. It was his display of control over me, time and time again. Now that the truth was out about exactly who was killing them, he would stop at nothing to make sure he was successful.

I also knew that *anyone* who touched Jade would deal with *me*. Father or not.

"We'll make a plan," I said. "Let's just get through this night first to make Isaiah happy."

"And since when do you care about making humans happy?" Adonis asked. "You're supposed to be the leader of Fearford, Mal. You're supposed to be their *king*. Our father declared as much when he sent you here. Jade's changing you for the worse, huh?"

31

A low growl rumbled the room around us. It took me a moment to realize it was coming from me.

"Relax, brother," he said. "I'm only kidding. If you want us to play nice with humans, we will. But Isaiah is arrogant. I don't like arrogant. I could rip that skinny man to shreds in two seconds if I wanted to."

"Get over yourself," Adeline said. "Isaiah has been the leader of this place, it has to be hard for him. He lost his father and he's trying his best to rule. You see what they have to work with here. It's not much. Why don't you at least try to show some respect."

Adonis smirked but didn't respond. Adeline always had a talent for shutting our brothers up.

"You can't actually think we're all going to that stupid human party tonight," one of the twins, Eli, said.

"If Esther wants us to make an appearance, that's what we'll do," I replied.

"You heard what they said. Something strange is happening at that thing. I don't want to be there when it goes down," Lucien added.

"Afraid of humans, Lucien?" I teased. Lucien frowned but kept his mouth shut, crossing his arms over his chest and leaning back onto the wall. "It will be nothing. Whatever weird party this is, we can handle it. It's just one night."

"Wait," Jade interrupted. "You're actually going to this party?"

"Why do you look surprised?" I asked.

She shook her head, biting her cheeks to hide her

smile. She still failed. "No reason," she started. "I just didn't really take you for a human party type of person."

"We're going strictly for business," I said. "I'm not staying long. One appearance and that's it."

"Great," she said. "I'll see you tonight then."

I watched her walk away, fighting every urge to follow her out that door. To never let her out of my sight.

But Jade could take care of herself here. I had to believe that.

"Yes you will," I mumbled after she was too far away to hear me.

The door closed behind me, and I was left with my family and Serefin.

Everyone stared at me like I was a stranger in front of them.

"What?" My voice echoed off the walls.

Everyone diverted their gaze then, quick to shuffle around the room in an effort to appear occupied.

Lucien was the only one that continued looking at me, chuckling silently while he shook his head. "You are a lion in a field of mice right now, brother," he said. "Don't starve yourself because you're too busy making friends."

CHAPTER 4
Jade

It was stupid that I was excited.

Stupid and naive and ignorant.

It was a stupid party that we were nearly *required* to attend as guests here. If anything, the night would test whether there was any hope for the humans and the fae getting along.

Was that Esther's plan? To see how quickly we would fail?

But it had been so long since I *actually* had a fun time. And even back home, I never hung out with other people. Besides Tessa, anyway.

My stomach tightened at the thought of my sister. If she knew what I was trying to do, would she hate me even more than she already did?

Shit... what *was* I trying to do?

Play *house* with Malachi? The Prince of Shadows?

My mind hadn't stopped wandering to his lips on mine. His hands wandering my body.

It had only been our second kiss, third if you want to count our wedding. But it felt so *right*. It felt *natural*.

I shook my head and kept walking. Where? I wasn't sure. Just being in this kingdom brought me a strange level of comfort. Walking through the rows of beat-down tents and half-built cottages.

These people didn't know luxury. They were fighters.

They were humans.

"You're not wearing that," Sadie said, interrupting my thoughts as she stepped into my path. She dragged her eyes up and down my tattered, dirty clothes.

Was she serious?

"I don't really have much to choose from, so this is the best it's going to get."

She stared at me for another second before clicking her tongue and saying, "Alright, this is the only time I'm going to do this. Follow me."

Sadie turned around and sauntered away before I could protest. I scrambled to keep up after her. I was decently fit, I would admit. Hours of running, hunting, and climbing back home kept me healthy and agile.

But Sadie was tall and she had at least four inches on me. Her strides were wide and graceful over the dirt ground.

We passed the run-down, makeshift tents of families one by one until we approached the end of the row. I almost thought we had passed it, or that Sadie had absolutely lost her mind, but right at the last second, she stopped and turned into a wooden shed.

I had to duck my head to step inside, but once we were in, it wasn't so bad. Sadie had clearly spent a lot of time and effort making this small area of dirt and wood feel like home.

I didn't blame her. Part of me even envied the small, carefully placed trinkets and items she held close to her heart. There had been times where I would have killed for a place like this, no matter how small or dirty.

A place that was *mine*.

Sadie crossed the room in two steps and began tugging on a large trunk, sliding it out of place to reveal a small hole in the ground.

"If you tell anyone about this," she warned when she caught me staring, "I'll kill you. I mean that."

She didn't mean it, but I nodded anyway.

"I can't imagine you have many safe-spaces around here," I responded, keeping my voice soft. I didn't want Sadie to be my enemy.

I knew exactly who she was.

She was just like me. Only she wasn't forced to marry the Prince of Shadows.

"Put this on," she said, throwing me a fresh pair of black clothes. "No arguing."

I held the clothes to my chest. "Why are you being nice to me?" I asked. "I figured you all hated the girl who married a fae."

Sadie shook her head. "We aren't stupid, Jade. We know about your father. We know he owed a debt to the King and that's why you were sent away to marry the Prince."

I couldn't hide the shock that was undoubtedly clouding my features. "What? How? Nobody knows about that," I said. *Not even Tessa.*

Tessa knew that I had to marry him, of course. She just didn't know the reasoning behind it. That my father had ruined everything for us, gambling and cheating until he had nothing left to give.

Nothing except me. But that was hardly an improvement.

"Fearford is one of the largest human cities. We have spies that give us intel. That little gem of information just happened to be some of it."

I couldn't believe it. Sadie knew that my dad had owed a debt to the King and that I was the one who repaid it.

Which meant Isaiah also knew.

"Don't worry," she interrupted, reading my thoughts. "Isaiah keeps his mouth shut. Nobody here cares, anyway. It's obvious that your Prince is totally obsessed with you. They might hate fae, but they can root for a love like that."

I scoffed. "No, no," I said. "It's not like that. He's saved my life a few times, that's it. Our marriage is political."

She squinted her eyes. "Right. That's why he was completely ballistic when we separated you two after you arrived."

Why didn't I remember that?

"I'm his wife in the eyes of the Paragon. He made a vow to protect me. Of course, he would be worried."

"Mmhm," she said. "We'll see how he reacts tonight when he sees you wearing something other than bloody rags. Now get changed. Use that bucket there to wash the dirt off yourself."

I could feel the heat of my blushing cheeks. I listened to her and quickly got moving while she turned her back to give me some privacy.

The clothes I was wearing practically peeled off my dirt-coated skin.

I removed layer by layer until they were nothing but a nasty pile on the floor. The bucket of water Sadie had gestured to looked clean. Not like I would complain, anyway. I had done this type of thing hundreds of times back home.

It was a far cry from the running water they had in Rewyth. The showers. The luxury.

But this is how us humans lived. I didn't make a sound as I quickly scrubbed my arms and legs, cleaning as much dirt off as possible.

By the time I was done, the water was nearly black. And I could actually see my skin again.

"Can I ask you something?" I asked her, breaking the growing silence between us.

She replied without turning around. "Sure."

I picked up the clothes she gave me and began stepping into them. "You said something earlier, about tonight's bonfire. That the fae here are treated differently or something like that. What did you mean?"

Sadie took a long, deep breath. She was hiding something. Hiding it, or keeping it inside of her because she didn't know how to let it out. One or the other.

"Esther has power, as you know. She's been part of this community since before I was ever born. I grew up knowing her, loving her. Supporting her. Her sacrifices never meant much to me."

"Sacrifices?" I asked, recalling my earlier conversation with Esther. She had mentioned something about sacrificing. "What does she sacrifice? Will that be tonight?"

"It will be tonight, yes." I watched her shake her head from behind. "Esther will kill me if I tell you."

My heart sank to my stomach. "It's me, isn't it?" I asked. "Esther saved my life because she wants to sacrifice me."

Sadie spun around to face me. Thank the Saints I had just finished putting the shirt on. "Seriously?" she asked. "You really think Esther would drag you all the way here to kill you?"

A sigh of relief escaped me. "I mean, I don't know! Plenty of weirder things have happened to me these past few weeks. And I don't know Esther like you do. I know her as the woman who abandoned Malachi, and as the woman who held a knife to my throat just days ago." I ran a hand over my neck.

Sadie relaxed an inch. "You're safe here, trust me," she mumbled. "But your friends should be careful."

"Why?" I asked. Desperation for answers began

creeping into my voice. "What's she planning to do with them, Sadie? What happens at these parties?"

"As long as they keep their mouths shut, nothing will happen. Really. I already told you the humans hate the fae. It wouldn't surprise me if Esther tried to use this event as some sort of power beacon. That's all."

My head spun. "So as long as my friends lay low, they'll be fine?" Sadie shrugged, as if she truly didn't know either way.

"I'm just trying to help you out," she admitted. "Human to human."

Sadie had a certain quality that made me want to trust her, but she also had a certain darkness that kept me wary. "Fine," I said. "I believe you."

"Besides," she added. "I think your fae are plenty capable of protecting themselves. This is a human kingdom, remember?"

I nearly laughed. "How could I forget?"

Sadie took a step back and turned her attention to the clothes I was wearing.

They were different than anything I had ever worn, back home or in Rewyth. The style in Rewyth had certainly been more formal than I was used to, but this...

My trousers were nearly form-fitted to my legs, leaving almost nothing to the imagination. My black blouse flowed around my arms, giving me plenty of room to breathe in the heat of the desert but exposing just enough skin at my chest to be flattering.

At least I thought so, anyway. But if Adeline had

taught me anything, it was that I had no sense of style whatsoever.

"Well?" I asked her. "How does it look?"

I don't care. I don't care. I don't care.

I waited for her response.

I cared.

"Damn, girl," she said. "Now I can see why you drive the Prince of Shadows crazy."

My stomach flipped, but I kept my features as straight as possible.

Nerves fluttered through every inch of my body.

What if the humans hated him? Not just him... what if they hated Adeline and Serefin? What if Mal's mother wasn't enough to convince them that we could stay? What if this entire thing was just a setup and Malachi's father would come for us any day?

This was supposed to be Malachi's kingdom. Not Isaiah's.

Then again, we weren't supposed to be here at all.

Sadie and I spent the rest of the day together, preparing for the night's event.

Keeping Malachi off my mind was entirely impossible, even with the strange pit in my stomach that told me something dreadful was coming.

CHAPTER 5
Malachi

"Why are we doing this?" Adonis asked me. "We could take over this kingdom right now without even breaking a sweat. Yet you're letting that Isaiah idiot talk to you like you're nothing."

"We have a plan, Adonis," my mother answered. "We should try getting along with the humans first. If we take over, your father will just invade and this will be another branch of Rewyth. We'll accomplish nothing, Malachi will wait ten more decades for a kingdom of his own, and this will all have been a waste. Besides, we need to keep Jade safe. We need the humans on our side."

Adonis rolled his eyes and Lucien let out a groan. I let my power flare in response, just enough to let them know I was still here.

My mother's eyes snapped to me. "Careful with that, son. If the humans know you possess that power, it won't help your case. Humans fear what they don't know. It's their nature."

"I don't need them to like me. I need them to like Jade. As long as she's safe here, I couldn't care less."

She shook her head. "You might be married legally, but it won't be enough. They need to believe that you two love each other if they're ever going to think that humans and fae can get along."

"I'm sure everyone already knows this was a setup. We won't fool them all. There's no logical way to explain how Jade possibly ended up married to me and wants to stay that way."

Adeline stepped forward. "They don't all know," she interjected. "That the wedding was forced, I mean. I heard a few humans talking earlier and they were completely shaken that Jade would choose to marry you. They have no idea that it wasn't her choice."

I reminded myself not to clench my fists.

"Either way, we stick with the plan," I said. "I won't just march into a city and take over like I run the place."

"But you do run the place, Mal," Serefin said from the back of the room. "This is your kingdom. Your father ordered you to rule."

"And I will. With time and in peace."

"You've grown soft," Adonis sneered. "This will never work. We don't have time."

"Show some respect," my mother interjected. "Your brother is making the right choice."

"Says who?" He spat. "You? No offense, *witch*, but that doesn't mean much to me."

Tension thickened the air. The ground grumbled beneath us, and this time, it wasn't from me. I looked to my mother, whose typically forest-green eyes had now turned black as night.

My attention turned to the ground beneath our feet, where the grass was dying inch by inch around my mother.

I could have sworn the air around her darkened, too.

Magic. She was using magic.

"Now," my mother said. "Your job is to go out there and make the humans like you. That's it. So don't screw this up for us, got it?"

My brothers nodded, but I knew they didn't have a choice. They had sworn a blood oath to my mother. They might not have been her sons, but she owned them.

I had only heard of a few other occasions when blood oaths had been taken. They were rare, requiring a powerful witch like my mother to be effective. Decades ago, there used to be rumors about entire armies who were sworn to one witch, everyone obeying the witch's every command. Those were just stories, but it could be entirely possible.

As long as the individual willingly took the blood oath, there was nothing that could be done to break it.

The blood oath would remain until the witch who originated it released them from the oath. It would be physically impossible to do anything against the oath swearer's will.

If it was her wish for them to obey tonight, they would have no choice but to oblige.

Saints, that made me happy.

"Hurry up now," my mother said. "The sun is already down and we don't want to keep them waiting. I'm sure everyone is dying to meet the mysterious fae."

"Right," I mumbled. "I'm sure they're just ecstatic."

I followed suit as she led the way, Adeline and Serefin staying close behind me.

I had never been one to care if others liked me or not. The Prince of Shadows had an entirely different reputation. Did the humans know that about me? Did they know I was the one their children feared? Had nightmares about?

Did they know I had killed hundreds of humans? That it took me less than a thought to drop a grown fae male to his knees with my power alone?

I doubted it. If they did, they would be fearing for their lives.

Not throwing a party.

We all had our wings hidden with glamour, just like the first time Jade had met us.

No need to scare them even more. *We were one of them*, my mother had said. *We were similar.*

And we were supposed to act that way tonight.

The deep vibration of music began creeping into the earth under my feet.

I wasn't a huge fan of music in the past. Music meant emotions. Emotions meant memories.

I couldn't afford memories.

But this music was accompanied by laughter and cheers. Dozens of voices chattered in the distance.

Adeline squealed in excitement. "Relax," I reminded her. "We might not even make it to the bonfire before we are forced out of here."

"Speak for yourself," she said. "Everyone likes me and you know it. And if they really hate the fae, I'll just lie and say I'm one of them." She flipped her hair over her shoulder and trotted forward toward the party.

"Your loyalty is astonishing, dear sister," I yelled after her.

Serefin put a hand on my shoulder as we continued to walk. "I can't say I have a good feeling about this," he whispered. "We're walking into a city of people who want us dead. That's never ended well for us."

"The difference is, Ser, these people don't stand a chance against us. We'll play along to give them what we want, and then we'll figure out how to get back at my father."

He nodded, and I knew he understood. Serefin always had my back, even if he knew I was being an idiot.

Which was more frequent than I'd like to admit.

We followed the small path of lanterns that lit a walkway to a large, open field. A massive fire, likely burning dozens of trees at the same time, illuminated the party ahead.

Makeshift tables and chairs scattered around the perimeter, making plenty of room for the humans to sit, talk, mingle. Food and drinks were being passed around freely, and it looked as if nearly the entire Kingdom of Fearford was already here.

I scanned the scene again, looking for any type of threat.

But all I saw was a chaotic, drunk group of humans.

And then I saw her.

Jade.

She was commanding the attention of everyone around her, whether she wanted to or not.

Jade was sitting on the end of a bench with a red drink in her hand. The glow of the nearby fire lit up her face as she talked and smiled. A few other girls sat around her, listening to every single word she said.

A couple of boys, probably Jade's age, stood behind them with the same level of concentration on Jade.

Only they had something else all over their faces, too.

I took a step forward.

"Don't," Ser said from behind me. "You heard your mother. You'll scare them."

"They're looking at her like she's a new toy."

"She's your wife, Mal. Not theirs. She can take care of herself."

Ser was right. I took a long, calming breath. If I stormed over there and shut them all up, the humans would hate me. My mother would despise me. And the night would be ruined.

I kept my mouth shut, clenched my jaw, and kept

following Ser to the other side of the bonfire. The side where Isaiah sat with Sadie and a few others.

"Welcome!" Isaiah said as he saw us. "Welcome friends! Thank you for coming!"

"Did we have a choice?" I responded.

I walked around the wooden table and took the seat right next to him, giving me a perfect view of the fire.

And of Jade, who was still oblivious to our arrival.

"We all have a choice," he continued. The others, including my brothers, took their seats at the same table. "But you made the right one. These parties are what the people of Fearford look forward to."

"What for?" I asked. "To sit around and stare at a fire?"

"Esther has been living with us since before I was even born. We have routines here. Rituals. There are other witches here who look up to her for peace and for guidance. They look up to both of us," he said.

"You're saying this is one of the witchy rituals?" I asked. I looked around again, but didn't see anything out of the ordinary.

"Don't make your arrogant judgements until you see it for yourself."

"Great," I mumbled to Ser. "I can't wait."

Isaiah chuckled coldly and took a long swig of his drink. "We might not be living in a palace, *Prince*, but humans do know how to have fun. Perhaps your wife can remind you sometime."

Hot anger rolled up my neck. "Don't talk about

Jade," I growled. "You don't know anything about her."

"And you do?"

"Yes. I do."

He shook his head and smiled. He looked just as juvenile as he acted. His eyes were shallow and ignorant. He may be living in poverty. He may struggle to feed his people. But he hadn't known real hardship.

He hadn't known real war.

I had known men like Isaiah my entire life. Men that thought they had everything figured out. Men that said a few words and expected the crowd to drink up every word. Men that had been handed their position in the world.

Men that had no idea what was coming.

"If I can have everyone's attention please!" He announced.

The humans obliged without another thought, ending their conversations and turning their attention toward Isaiah.

"Thank you, thank you. We've been hosting these parties once a month for years now, and I could not be happier that I get to continue on my father's legacy with the same traditions." The crowd fell into still silence. "But we have recently been given the chance to carry on something that my father always wanted. To unite the humans and fae."

I looked through the crowd or orange glowing humans. Some of them made sounds of disgust, others sat quietly and continued to stare at Isaiah as if he were their savior.

When my eyes fell on Jade, she was already staring at me. Her brows were drawn together, and I could tell that she had tightened the grip on her drink.

I didn't break eye contact as Isaiah continued. "As some of you may have heard, we have had a few guests stop by. Malachi, will you please stand up."

"It's *Prince* Malachi," Serefin yelled from the table, which caused a roar of hollers from the crowd.

I ignored them all and stood, letting the humans know who their enemy was. What we looked like.

"For centuries," he continued, "the humans and the fae have been rivals. The humans have starved while the fae have feasted. We, as humans, have nothing to offer. Nothing to give. Not to them."

Hundreds of human eyes stared at me. I did not move.

"Prince Malachi and his friends are fae from Rewyth. They come here to unite our lands, bring us riches, and save us from poverty," he preached, pure confidence lacing every word.

I physically flinched at his words. How *idiotic* they were.

My father had no intentions of following up with this deal. Even I could see that. The humans had spent centuries in suffering, and that wasn't going to change just because I waltzed in here with a human.

"But Prince Malachi has come to help us. He has

come to finally put a stop to this ridiculous feud between human and fae."

"How?" someone yelled. "How will he be able to help us?"

Isaiah turned to me as he answered. "That's what our friends are here to help us discover, isn't that right?"

I clenched my jaw. If I opened my mouth to respond, he wouldn't like what would come out.

"Enjoy yourselves!" he continued after a couple of seconds. He turned back to the crowd and raised a drink. "Eat, drink, dance. We're one family here at Fearford, so let's make our guests feel welcome!"

Isaiah was quickly pulled to the side, talking to the dozens of people that practically begged for his attention.

And with that, the music started up again. Any hatred the humans had felt toward us seemed to dissipate as everyone moved around the fire, swaying to the beats of the music.

A sharp pang of envy bolted through my chest. It had been decades since I had fun like that. Saints, it was an entire other lifetime.

Before the wars. Before the guilt. Before the marriages.

And before all the death.

If these people knew all the things I had done, they wouldn't let their guard down around me. Around any of the fae, for that matter.

Serefin handed me another drink. It was obviously

nothing compared to the drinks we had for the fae in Rewyth, but perhaps if I drank enough it would eventually take the edge off.

If that were even possible.

"How long do you think he'll keep that act up?" Serefin asked when I sat back down.

"What act?"

"The act where he thinks he's in charge."

I choked down a laugh. "We've known plenty of men just like him. He'll do anything he can to appear like he's in charge, but when shit starts going in the hole, he'll be looking for someone else the people can blame. I'm not sure what his angle is here, but I don't like it."

"Yeah. Me either."

"He wants something with Jade. I can feel it. I just don't know what."

Serefin considered my words. "Would your mother know?"

I shook my head. "Even if she did, she wouldn't tell me. She acts like she's loyal to us, but she's lived with these humans for decades now. We have to keep our eyes open."

"Agreed, brother."

We both relaxed in our seats and observed the scene of the bonfire. My other brothers seemed to be doing the same.

Adeline rushed up to me and Serefin. It was then that I realized she had stepped away at some point. Her hair blew all over the place as she approached, and she had a look on her face that made me think she was actually enjoying herself.

"Come dance!" she said, rushing up to Serefin and I and grabbing each of us by the arm. "Come dance with me!"

"Absolutely not," I answered as Serefin mumbled his own declining words.

"Come on!" she whined. "It's a party! You all look so grumpy over here sitting by yourselves. Everyone's having fun!"

"Dancing with the humans isn't fun, Adeline," Adonis chimed in from behind me. "It's embarrassing."

Adeline brushed his comment off with the wave of her hand.

"Fine," she said. "I'll make Jade dance with me."

Nobody responded, but the hair on my neck stood up at the mention of Jade's name.

Adeline trotted away, through the crowd, until she was out of sight. Serefin kept his eyes glued on the crowd, too. Ready to interfere if needed.

Always protecting Jade.

"At least one of us can be friendly," I muttered to Ser.

He laughed and took another drink. "Your sister could solve the entire nation's problems in one afternoon. I'm certain of it."

I laughed with him but couldn't get past the growing pit in my stomach. I scanned the crowd, looking for that familiar black hair of hers. Why did I even let her out of my sight in the first place?

But she would be fine with Adeline.

These were just humans, after all. Nothing was going to happen to her.

I needed to relax.

Just as I was about to turn around and give up on the entire idiotic party with the humans, Jade's laugh rippled through the air.

Every muscle in my body tensed.

Adeline held tightly to her hands as she swung her around a small circle. A few other humans circled them, laughing and drinking as they moved to the beats of the music.

Serefin laughed quietly next to me.

"What?" I asked, snapping out of my trance.

"You're in big trouble, brother."

I shook my head. "I don't know what you're talking about."

Ser leaned in, placing his elbows on his knees, and said, "You know exactly what I'm talking about. You can't forget that she's a human. I get that you wanted to save her life before, and that made you protective. She might be your wife in Rewyth, but the humans might not see it the same way."

"I've never cared about what the humans think."

"I know that. But you care about Jade. It's obvious to anyone who pays attention to the way you two look at each other. All I'm saying is that humans will look at this union as an abuse of power."

"Adeline said the humans supported our union."

Ser shook his head and leaned back in his chair. He

had an aloof appearance, and only I knew him well enough to know it was a facade. Serefin might look relaxed and laid back, but he was watching every single person at this party.

He had been watching me, too. And Jade.

I trusted Serefin. I trusted what he had to say to me.

"Adeline hasn't been watching them the same way I have. Look over there," he said, pointing to the darker edge of the clearing.

I followed Serefin's gaze and my power immediately rumbled in my body, letting me know it was still there. A group of men, now including Isaiah, were huddled in a small circle, heads down, whispering. Their tense body language and clenched fists told me everything I needed to know. For whatever reason, they weren't happy.

One individual in particular pointed his finger at Isaiah, yelling something I couldn't hear over the pounding music.

"Those are the type of people we have to look out for. Not the ones laughing and dancing."

I nodded. Serefin was right. We weren't looking in the right places.

"Should we go over there and see what's going on?" I asked.

"Absolutely not. But your call," he answered.

I moved to stand from my chair but was immediately cut off by a small group of girls running up to where my brothers and I were sitting.

"Come dance!" they chirped. One of the tall,

blonde humans grabbed my brothers Eli and Fynn by the wrists and pulled them to their feet. If it weren't for her shockingly low-cut shirt, I'm sure they would have objected. But instead, they let the cluster of girls pull them to dance in the crowd.

As the moon rose in the sky, people began to let loose. More and more men added to the song of flutes and fiddles. Laughs became louder and more carefree. The energy electrified, a palpable tension in the air.

My other brothers were next. In the swarm of the crowd, they had little choice in the matter. After a few objections, they also were swallowed into the sea of dancers.

I scanned the crowd, looking for Adeline. She had to be up to this.

Ser looked to me for help when two girls grabbed each of his arms, but I only shrugged.

They wanted us to mingle with the humans, anyway.

The girls cheered and clapped as he, too, rose to his feet and followed them into the sea.

But nobody grabbed me. Nobody tried to convince me to dance.

Smart humans. Perhaps they *did* have an idea of who I was.

I scanned the crowd again, almost laughing at how awkward Serefin looked as the crowd tried to get him to move his hips from left and right.

"You're missing all the fun," Jade's voice made me jump.

"Who says watching isn't the best part?" I replied.

Jade smiled. She was breathing heavily, probably from running and cheering with the crowd. Her eyes looked differently than I had seen them before.

They looked alive.

"What?" she asked, stepping closer. "You're too good to have a fun time?" She stood directly in front of me, almost close enough to touch. "It's a party, Malachi."

She leaned forward, placing an arm on either side of me. I could smell the liquor on her breath, warm and sharp. "Don't you want to come dance with me?"

Now she was definitely close enough to touch. Close enough that I could cover her mouth with mine in a second.

But I didn't budge. Didn't blink.

"No," I answered, even though my body was telling me something different. "I don't want to dance."

"Really?" she asked. Her eyes flickered down to my lips, lingering for only a moment. "You won't come dance with me? Your wife?"

"Dancing isn't really my thing."

She nodded and stood back up, allowing me to finally take a breath.

"Fine," she said. "Suit yourself."

And with that, Jade Farrow walked away, back into the sea of humans. I watched her until she was too deep in the crowd, but every inch of me could still feel her presence.

And every inch of me needed more.

CHAPTER 6
Jade

Damn. I hadn't drank this much in a *very* long time.

Like, *ever*.

I knew I was teasing Malachi. But I also knew he liked it.

And that was addicting.

Even if he wouldn't come dance with me.

The music moved through my body, commanding each of my movements. The summer sun had set long ago, but the heat of the crowd sent beads of sweat rolling down my neck.

I didn't care if I looked like an idiot. I closed my eyes and tilted my head backward, letting the beat of the drums hit the deepest parts of my soul.

I wasn't the only one, either. Dozens of humans were doing the exact same thing, either alone or in the arms of their loved ones. Two bodies melded into one.

It was euphoric.

Bodies bumped into mine from every direction, but I didn't mind. Not as we all moved however the music wanted.

When two large hands grabbed me around the waist from behind, I stepped forward slightly. I didn't turn around. I figured my body language was clear enough.

Apparently I was wrong.

The hands grabbed me again, pulling me backward against a sweaty male body.

And it wasn't Malachi.

"Come on, baby," he whispered in my ear. His breath reeked of liquor and smoke. "A girl like you doesn't need to dance alone."

I shoved the hands away once again, saying, "Not interested."

It wasn't until the grimy hands grabbed me *again* that I became pissed off.

But when I turned to shove the loser one last time, my jaw dropped.

Malachi's power rumbled through the ground, although I'm sure the humans were too drunk to notice anything out of the ordinary. He was on the loser within a second, grabbing his shirt collar and holding tightly. "You're done here," was all he said.

The grabby man's face changed entirely as he stared at Malachi with wide eyes.

"I wasn't doing anything, man," he muttered.

"You touched my wife," Malachi growled. "You

should be happy that you still have your hands. And I'm not your *man*."

I would have said something. I would have intervened, I would have told Malachi to put the guy down. But I was frozen in place.

Me and everyone else who was now watching.

Malachi must have realized this, too. He let go of the man, who staggered backward in fear, and rolled his shoulders back.

The music still played, but everyone was staring at us.

At Malachi.

"You really know how to cause a scene," I said.

Malachi shrugged. "He shouldn't have done that."

"He just wanted to dance."

"He wanted a lot more than *a dance,* princess."

Heat creeped up my cheeks. I glanced at the faces around us, most of which had small hints of fear written all over them.

Malach's outburst was going to ruin the entire plan.

I held out my hand to him. "I suppose you'll have to take his place, then," I teased.

My heart was pounding in my ears. I had been drinking, yes, but that was no worse than the usual effect Malachi had on me. Combining the two, though, was going to be dangerous.

But right now, I didn't care one bit.

He mumbled something under his breath before stepping forward, but he didn't take my hand. He yanked my wrist firmly and sent my body stumbling into his.

Malachi caught me around the waist and I wrapped my arms around his neck to support myself.

"Fine," he whispered, close enough for only me to hear. "But just one dance."

A few people around us snickered and giggled before returning to their own dance movements, adjusting their paces to the now slower beat of the music.

"You can't go around scaring the shit out of people, you know," I said. "It's not a great way to make friends."

Malachi took a deep breath, his chest touching mine as it rose and fell.

"What if I don't want to make friends?"

"I don't think your mother would like that very much."

"And what if I don't care about what my mother thinks?"

The intensity in his gaze made me shut my mouth. I had been this close to Malachi a handful of times now, but my body reacted like it was the first. His hand on my waist slid to my lower back, his fingers brushing the exposed skin in a gentle touch.

"Do you really think this plan will work?" I asked, breathing heavily and desperate to distract myself from his touch.

Malachi smirked. "I don't know. I've never spent

time with humans before. I have no idea what they will or will not fall for."

"Like a fae and a human actually getting along?"

"Right," he said. "Like that."

"Well they're all watching us now," I teased. I unclasped my hands from around his neck and twirled a finger through his thick, curly hair. My heart was beating faster. Stronger. "We could convince them."

Malachi stiffened at my touch. For a second, I thought he was going to pull away.

His eyes darkened, but his grip on my waist didn't falter.

"Are you sure this is a good idea?" he asked.

With my next words, I was certain I was drunk.

"What? You've kissed me before. I even thought you liked it, too."

The corner of Malachi's mouth turned upward, but he quickly recovered. "And what if I did?"

"Then I suppose humans and fae can get along, after all."

We spun in circle after circle, dancing more intimately than I had ever danced with anyone before.

Malachi took a deep breath and turned his attention up to the night sky. His throat bobbed once, and when he returned his gaze, his eyes had changed entirely.

Something like desire dripped heavily over every feature.

A look that made my stomach flip.

Malachi leaned down, close enough that our lips

barely brushed when he whispered, "If you want me to kiss you in front of all these people, princess, you'll have to ask me nicely."

My breath hitched. Another bead of sweat rolled down my chest. "You want me to ask you to kiss me?"

"Mmmhm," he hummed. He no longer hid his amusement.

"Fine," I hummed back, lifting my chin so my eyes met his. "Will you kiss me, dear husband?"

Malachi laughed quietly, and the vibrations of it erupted through my body.

"Anything you desire will be yours, dear wife," he whispered, and before I could take another breath, his mouth crashed into mine.

Our bodies moved together under the night sky of Fearford. The music still blared around us, but the only thing I could hear was the sound of my own heartbeat as Malachi kissed me, deep and passionate. His hands didn't leave my body, only held me tighter against him as if he would never let go.

And I didn't want him to let go.

I kissed him back, letting my hands wander from his hair to his shoulders to his back, where strong black wings should have been. I wished then that he wasn't using glamour, that I could see the wings that had been wrapped around us before.

Malachi smiled against my mouth.

"What?" I mumbled as I pulled back just enough to look at his face.

"I know what you're thinking," he breathed.

"Oh yeah? And what's that?"

Malachi glanced around us, as if he were checking to see who was looking, before he dropped his glamour. It was a bold move. His dark wings were tucked in tightly, but they were still massive as I looked up at them.

"I was right, wasn't I?" he said, moving in to place his hot mouth against my neck, my collarbone.

I closed my eyes again and held onto him tightly as he continued to move us to the beat of the music.

I felt...I felt carefree. I felt giddy. I didn't remember the last time I had felt this happy. I certainly never expected to feel happy with him.

With the Prince of Shadows.

But here we were.

Malachi pressed his forehead against mine, our breaths blending together as we danced through the crowd.

Until a blood-curdling scream split through the air.

CHAPTER 7
Jade

The music stopped playing immediately. Malachi and I jumped apart, ready for whatever problem we were about to face.

"What's going on?" I asked.

Panic crept into my chest as I looked at the crowd around us. Well, looked *back* at the crowd around us.

Everyone had stopped what they were doing and now stared at Malachi, whose massive black wings still flared around his body.

They hadn't seen fae wings before. They certainly hadn't seen Malachi's wings before. And they looked mortified.

"They're just wings," I announced. My desperation to resolve the situation only increased with every passing second.

Malachi's glamour was back in an instant, covering any trace of a fae appearance that had slipped through.

"Demon," one of them muttered. My blood ran cold.

"Don't be ridiculous," Malachi replied. "They're just wings."

"Black wings," another person mumbled from the depths of the crowd.

"You knew we were fae," he continued. "What did you expect?"

I wanted to reach a hand out to him, to tell everyone he wasn't someone they should fear.

But who would I be then? Just moments ago, I was kissing him in the crowd. But this was the same fae I had been forced to marry. The same fae who had killed thousands.

He might have been my husband. But he was still a stranger to them.

"Let's just go," I said, stepping toward him and lowering my voice.

"No," another voice chimed in. Malachi's mother. "Don't leave. You are our guests here." She emerged slowly from the fae end of the crowd. The people shifted to make way for her as she walked toward us.

Her eyes blared into Malachi with the look of a disappointed mother. I wanted to laugh in her face.

I knew that look all too well. And I also knew when it wasn't deserved.

"It was my fault," I interrupted. "I made him do it. I didn't think anyone was paying attention."

Malachi's mother only shook her head. "It's nobody's fault, dear. The fae deserve to be themselves.

They shouldn't have to hide who they really are, especially here. Right?" she asked.

Most of the humans just stared at each other in awe, others still looked at Malachi in disgust.

"Show them," she said to Malachi, and now to his brothers who were approaching from their own spots in the crowd. "Show them what you all really look like."

Malachi began to object, but Lucien, who had been lurking this entire time, beat him to it. He dropped his glamour, revealing the wicked silver wings I had grown to resent.

The same wings that carried me through the sky just a few nights ago. I hadn't forgotten.

The crowd gasped as soon as they realized what they were looking at.

Adonis followed, and so did the twins. Serefin and Adeline now stood behind Malachi, though, waiting for his move.

"It's okay, son," Mal's mother cooed. "Show them who you are."

Malachi's throat bobbed. I knew he didn't care about what these humans thought, but he would try. *For me.*

He would try to get the humans to like him.

Which meant they couldn't fear him.

Malachi's eyes shifted to mine. Those beautiful, dark eyes. The eyes that held decades of secrets, secrets that I would never unearth from the depths.

Malachi didn't care about the humans' opinions.

He cared about mine. I was now his window into the human world.

I nodded once.

And his midnight black wings reappeared.

The crowd collectively gasped again. A child screamed in the distance.

You would have thought they were staring straight into the face of a monster.

Maybe they were.

"Why are they black?" an older woman asked. "Your wings?"

Malachi opened his mouth to respond, but his mother answered for him. "We don't know," she said. "They were like that when he was born."

The older woman, with white hair and wrinkles around her eyes, smiled slyly. How many lifetimes had these fae lived? When all us humans had was this one, precious life? "It can't be good, boy. It can't be a good omen."

She stepped forward toward Malachi, causing me to step back so she would have room. She placed a hand on his shoulder. He stiffened, although I was probably the only one who noticed.

The crowd silenced as everyone waited for her next words. But she leaned in close to Malachi, who graciously bowed so he could hear, and whispered.

It could have only been a sentence or two.

But Malachi's entire posture changed.

The woman turned, and I thought she was going to

walk back into the crowd. But she stopped directly in front of me.

Malachi acted as if he would interfere, but nobody moved an inch.

"You," she hissed, pointing a curved finger at my chest. "You are the one. Your mother told us you would be coming soon."

"What?" I whispered to her.

"The peacemaker. We've been waiting for you."

Peacemaker? My head was spinning. How many drinks had this woman had?

"My mother is dead," I whispered. "You must be thinking of someone else."

The woman looked to Malachi's mother, who just gave her a knowing glance. "You should have brought her here sooner," she said. Esther simply bowed her head.

What in the Saints was she talking about?

I looked to Malachi for any inkling of help, but he looked equally as lost.

Gratefully, however, the woman had lost interest. She walked back into the crowd, which parted like she was fire. And she didn't look back.

Adeline was the one who spoke next. "You don't need to be afraid," she yelled. "We aren't here to harm any of you. We just want peace!"

I cringed internally. They would never believe that. Saints, *I* would have never believed that. It had taken the fae saving my life multiple times for me to believe that they didn't actually want every single human being dead.

It took me getting to know Adeline and Serefin.

And Malachi.

I still wasn't so sure about Malachi's brothers, especially Lucien.

The humans didn't have that same chance that I did. They weren't forced to move to Rewyth and see it all for themselves. They simply had to take the fae's word for it.

The word of their enemy.

"Adeline," I said, stepping forward. Her sharp ears stuck out of her long, bouncy hair. She wanted them to like her. I knew that. But they were never going to give her a chance.

And somewhere deep inside of my heart, that hurt. It hurt for her.

"No, Jade," she said, emotion leaking into every word. "They need to understand. We came here to help. Malachi came here to help."

"Then let her go!" another stranger shouted.

My heart was pounding again, but this time I knew it wasn't from the liquor.

"She's not a captive!" Adeline shouted back. "She's Malachi's wife!"

"Only because you forced her into it!" the voice persisted.

Malachi was at a loss for words. His brothers weren't much help, either, as they snickered in the background.

Because it was the truth. There was nothing they could say.

"Jade?" Adeline asked, tears swelling in her eyes. I opened my mouth to say something but nothing came out. What could I possibly say, anyway? That they were wrong? That I willingly entered this marriage?

I couldn't say any of that.

I shook my head at Adeline, mouth wide open. The look of disappointment and hurt on her face was one I would never forget.

"Well," Esther interrupted. "Since we're all here, I suppose we should get the real event of the evening started. Isaiah?"

Isaiah appeared in the crowd, and a small clearing formed around him.

It was then that I noticed a small, makeshift altar at one of the vacant wooden tables.

As if it were even possible, the silence of the crowd increased.

"Come here," she demanded, power dripping from her every move. Her usual lightness had been replaced. She was nearly unrecognizable. The energy between us all darkened instantly, and only continued to darken as the four brothers moved toward Esther, unable to disobey.

Did the others know they had sworn a blood oath?

Esther was wielding a power so strong, these four fae men could not even look away. Neither could I, I noticed. It was as if we were all entranced, watching this interaction.

The twins made it to her first, stopping in unison before her with Lucien and Adonis behind them.

Malachi was a statue beside me, his radiating body heat the only indication that he was still there.

"Many of you know about us witches and our rituals, but I'll give a quick history lesson for our new guests," she started. "We witches have been losing our power for many decades now. This isn't news to anyone."

A few people in the crowd nodded. How many of them were witches?

"What is new," she continued, "is the recent finding that small sacrifices can protect our magic, even if it is just temporary."

I didn't dare move. I didn't even risk a glance at Malachi. If he was feeling an inch of the dread I was feeling, his face would break me.

"This small sacrifice is something we have been doing every few months for decades now. And today," she motioned to the brothers, "with the help of these men, our magic will be protected once again."

The only sign of resistance was Lucien's clenched fists. Did they know this would be part of the oath? Was this the first time they had been used for a sacrifice?

"Your hand, please," she said. One by one, the brothers stepped forward.

And one by one, she sliced a small blade across their palms, squeezing drops of blood onto the makeshift altar.

"Did you know this was happening?" I whispered to Malachi, not sure if he could even hear me.

He mumbled something in response but it was barely audible over the ringing in my ears.

"You are all very generous for your sacrifices," Esther said to the boys. "And the Saints will thank you for this."

The fire cracked and spewed behind us, making me jump.

"It's done, then," Isaiah said eventually, clapping his hands. "Once again, Esther graces us with protection. Because of this sacrifice, we can all rest our heads this evening knowing that the Saints are on our side."

"Saints, save us," the crowd murmured in one demonic, unified voice.

Malachi leaned down and whispered in my ear. In my drunken state, I even thought I imagined it.

"Saints, save us."

CHAPTER 8

Malachi

Adonis avoided eye contact, staring down at his dusty shoes. He wasn't usually one to keep his mouth shut.

He must've learned a thing or two.

"If you have something to say just spit it out already," I spat. We had been sitting in this dark, musty room for half an hour now. Esther demanded we meet with her in private, but that was before she left to talk to her *beloved* Isaiah.

Whom I was becoming increasingly less fond of.

Adonis shook his head and turned his eyes toward the ceiling, smiling to himself. "You just had to ruin it for us, didn't you?" he asked.

"Ruin what, exactly? Esther's genius plan to save us all?"

He leaned forward, staring at me with hidden anger in his eyes. An anger that he and I shared. "She's trying to help us. You can't get over yourself long enough to look past your mommy issues. Esther is the only one that can bring down our father."

"You have to believe her," I argued. "You swore a blood oath, remember? Are we going to pretend that the *ritual* tonight was normal?"

"A blood oath makes me obey her commands, idiot. Not believe everything she says. If Esther thinks a stupid ceremony with our blood is going to keep this entire kingdom safe, so be it."

"I can't believe we came here," I mumbled. "This isn't going to help anything."

"There you go again, not seeing the bigger picture. Esther has a point. You have to be patient, brother. We might be stuck here kissing the ass of a bunch of humans, but this gives us time. Time to wait for our father to screw up. To make mistakes. He'll be going absolutely ballistic without us soon. And as soon as he lashes out..."

"We make a move."

Adonis nodded.

"But do you really think he won't just march here and kill us? Or send assassins, at least?"

Adonis shook his head again. "Doubtful. He'll be sitting in Rewyth, waiting for the day we all come walking back in there."

"He sent me to rule this kingdom for a reason, Adonis. He has to know something we don't."

Esther's voice trailed in from outside the door. Adonis stiffened in his chair before whispering, "And that is where your mother comes in. Try listening for once."

I clenched my fists to keep from lashing out again. Adonis was the smarter of my brothers. If he wanted me to listen to what Esther had to say, I could at least try.

After decades of spying on my family, she better have some decent insight. Especially after using my brothers' blood for a *sacrifice*.

She mumbled something else outside before opening the door, her long, gray, hair blowing across her face as she shut it behind her.

"Thank you boys for your patience," she said. "Busy night."

"Indeed," Adonis mumbled back. I stayed quiet.

"I think that went quite well, actually," she said, "despite the little scene toward the end."

"You mean despite the humans freaking out? Or despite you cutting each of my brothers for their blood?" I spoke up.

"You can't judge them for fearing the unknown," she continued, ignoring my second statement. "It's human nature."

"And how would you know that," I pushed. "Considering you're clearly not human."

Esther paused where she stood near the wall and simply tilted her chin. "You're angry," she stated.

I rolled my eyes. Of course I was angry. I was royally *pissed*. I had been forced out of Rewyth, turned into a damned spectacle, and walked all over by this Isaiah guy who thought he ran the place.

Shit was going to change around here. And soon.

"Yes," I started. "I am angry. And I'm getting tired of these humans treating us like we can't kill them all in five seconds."

"Threats aren't going to help you," she said.

"I think my rule over Fearford would be much more... effective."

"Why?" she asked. "Because you have a great gift? Because your wings are black?"

"Because I'm the heir to the throne," I reminded her.

"Yes," she continued. "The fae throne. Not the human throne."

I could have laughed out loud. Everyone knew the humans didn't have a throne. Not a real one, anyway. They were fighting to survive every single day. What seat did they have at the table of war, trading, and politics?

"Then what are we doing here? My father sent me here to rule. He *gave* me this kingdom."

Esther began pacing. "Honestly, Malachi, if you really think forcing these humans into submission and using them as servants will help you get anywhere in this life, be my guest. But you're not thinking clearly. Your father wants this land. He sent you here because he thought you would fail."

I took a deep breath and tried to calm down. "That's ridiculous. He knows I won't fail."

"He was counting on it!" she replied. For the first time since I had seen my mother again, she was losing her temper. "He sent you here because he knew the humans would fear you. He knew you would force them all to submit and it would be more proof that the humans and the fae cannot get along."

"Why would he care? He just wants this land for himself without punishment from the Paragon."

"Exactly," she continued. "If you force the humans into submission and the Paragon hears about this, you're the one that gets punished. Not him."

My mind raced through each of her words.

"But if we can get the humans to like you, to live peacefully with you and possibly even accept you into their community..."

"The Paragon will never know."

"The Paragon will never know," she repeated.

Shit. I didn't dare look at Adonis. I knew he would have that arrogant look splattered all over his face.

He was right. Esther did know what she was doing.

"And Jade?" I asked. "What about her?"

Esther and Adonis locked eyes for a second before she answered. "Jade will not be harmed."

"Well I would seriously hope not," I boomed. "But I'm glad that's cleared up."

Esther stepped forward and finally took a seat with Adonis and me. "Look," she started. "I know you heard what that elder said at the party. About Jade being the peacemaker."

I eyed my mother. "Was I supposed to believe anything that woman said?" I asked.

"Maybe not from her, but you should listen to me. Jade is special. I told you this before and I meant it. She's written in dozens of scriptures from the Saints. We've been waiting on her for decades now, Malachi."

"You're kidding, right? Jade's just a human. Her father is a drunk. She's not part of any crazy story the elders might have told you."

"She's special, Malachi. There's a reason these boys are sworn to protect her." I opened my mouth to respond but quickly shut it. My brothers had taken blood oaths to protect Jade. But that didn't mean that she was some special descendent of the Saints or the girl the elders had been waiting on.

Adonis spoke next. "Listen to her, Malachi. She's telling the truth."

"Is this what you wanted to talk to me about?" I asked. "You both wanted to corner me here to tell me that my wife isn't the person I think she is? Do you hear how ridiculous that sounds?"

"She might look like a regular human to you now, Malachi, but she isn't. Let me talk to her. Let me work with her. I can figure out if my elders were right about everything."

It sounded absurd. It sounded like Esther had absolutely lost her mind and was taking my brothers with her.

"Have you talked to Jade about any of this? Does she know?"

Esther sighed. "She knows I saved her life. And she's a smart girl. She has to know something."

Jade wasn't going to take this well. She wanted her life back. She had made that very clear to me even before hearing my mother's conspiracies. She was surviving for now, but I knew she would leave at the first chance she had to get back to her family.

If they would take her back, that is.

"Fine," I said, standing from my chair. "Do whatever you want. I can't make the humans like me if they already have their minds made up."

"Just lay low for a while," she said. "I'll handle it."

I nodded once to Adonis and left the room, back into the night.

Saints. What was happening? What had this all come to? Two months ago, I would have been living another boring, ignorant day in Rewyth, doing whatever my father asked of me. I was fine.

And then Jade changed everything.

I had no idea where she stood with her feelings for me. Tonight had been fun, but how would she feel in the morning? Would she still accept me in front of all the humans in the daylight?

"Brother, wait up!" Adonis yelled from behind me. He jogged to catch up with me, and I didn't slow a single step. "We need to talk," he started.

"I think we've talked enough," I mumbled.

"No," he said, grabbing my arm and forcing me to stop walking. "We need to talk about the King. We need to talk about our father."

That interested me. "What about him?"

Adonis looked at our surroundings and pulled me further into the darkness of the path we were walking before he whispered. "We know you want to kill him."

My stomach dropped. "Saints, Adonis, you can't just go around saying shit like that."

"We want to help you, Malachi."

"Even having this conversation could get us killed for treason. You know we can't kill him," I said, even though I had been dreaming about this very thing since we left Rewyth.

Since he allowed his guards to harm Jade.

I stopped myself from shivering as memories of Jade's ripped up back flashed through my mind.

They had whipped her. Yes, they were all going to die.

"Why would you want to help me, anyway?" I asked.

"We have our reasons," he stated.

"We?"

"Us, your brothers."

I wanted to believe Adonis. I really did. But decades of lying and sneaking around with my father had taught me to be smarter than that.

"If you want to kill our father, go right ahead," I said. This conversation had already gone on too long.

"We need your help," he called after me. "You know we have to do this together, brother."

"We should be happy if he lets us all live," I sneered. "Especially after you've been working with *her*."

"He'll never know. He has no way of suspecting that we're working with Esther."

"And you can be sure about that?"

Adonis closed his eyes and shook his head. "No," he answered. "I can't be sure about anything. But we're not just going to sit back and let him run our kingdom to ruins."

I had to admit, I had never seen Adonis so passionate about Rewyth. In fact, I never thought that any of my brothers actually cared about the kingdom.

I wanted to believe him, but my instincts told me to keep my guard up.

"Fine," I answered. "I'll help you. But I still don't trust her. And nobody else can know about this."

He smiled. "Agreed."

And with that, Adonis was gone.

Leaving me with a nauseating wave of dread.

I should have gone straight to bed. I shouldn't have pushed the boundaries any further.

But my mind wasn't going to rest until I talked to Jade.

I waited until Adonis was entirely out of sight before taking a left turn, straight toward where I knew Jade was staying.

CHAPTER 9
Jade

I was almost back to my poor excuse of a housing facility when I heard strong footsteps following me in the darkness.

"Not now," I yelled toward whoever it was. "I'm not in the mood!"

"I didn't mean to make things difficult for you," a voice said. *Isaiah's voice.*

I stopped walking and turned around. After the tension at the party and the blood sacrifice, I wasn't in the mood for this. "What do you want, Isaiah?"

He held his hands out in defense. "I just want to talk," he said.

"Can it wait until tomorrow?" I asked. My body was exhausted from the evening, and I wanted nothing more than to slip into bed and sleep for three days straight.

"It will be quick," he insisted. "I promise."

"Fine," I stated. "What's this about?" My words

came out sassier than I wanted them to, but I didn't have the strength to care.

"Just checking in," he said. He clasped his hands behind his back and walked toward me slowly, his boots grinding on the dirt beneath our feet. "Tonight didn't go exactly as planned."

A long breath escaped me. "No," I agreed. "It didn't."

"Is Malachi always this...aggressive?"

The question alone sent a rush of emotion through my body. "Malachi is the Prince of Shadows. I believe he can act however he likes."

"Fair enough," he answered carefully. "But still. I can't help but wonder how scary that must be for you."

What was he getting at?

"It's not scary at all, actually," I said, suddenly feeling defensive. "People who fear him just don't know who they're dealing with. He would never hurt me."

"Right," Isaiah continued. "Of course he wouldn't."

"What's that supposed to mean?"

Isaiah stepped closer. He was close enough now that I could see the golden freckles that spotted his tan skin.

"What I'm trying to say is that you're safe here, Jade. You don't have to pretend. We can protect you from *them*. From the fae. If you want protection, that is."

I shook my head. "They have never hurt me,

Isaiah." *Most of them, anyway.* "Malachi has saved my life on more than one occasion."

"But you're still married," he continued.

"Yes," I breathed.

"And you didn't want to get married, did you, Jade?"

My heart was pounding in my chest, so loud Isaiah could likely hear it. Of course I hadn't wanted to get married. Getting married to Malachi had been my worst nightmare just a few weeks ago. But why? Because I thought he would kill me? Because I thought they would take Tessa if I didn't go? Because I had a family to look out for? A selfish father to save?

I shook my head. I hadn't wanted to get married. But this marriage had turned into something I could have never expected.

Something that felt terrifyingly real.

"Look," Isaiah continued after I failed to respond to his question, "I know you're in a tough situation. But I know what you really want, Jade. I can help you."

"Oh really?" I laughed. "And what is it that I really want?"

Isaiah took another step closer. I stepped back, but my body hit the wall of the building behind me. I took a deep breath and reminded myself not to panic. Isaiah wasn't the enemy.

Right?

"You want freedom. You want to go home to your sister and your father, and you want to forget about all of this."

Well, he was right about some of it.

I would kill to go back to Tessa. To apologize. To let her know that I was still the same person and that I would do anything to protect her.

She was the only family I had, and after our last interaction, she was afraid. Of Malachi or of me, it didn't matter.

It all just seemed too far out of reach.

"You can't help me with that," I sighed. "Nobody can."

"And that's where you're wrong, Jade," Isaiah said. His eyes were wide and wild. Isaiah looked manic, like he would lose his mind at any second.

I didn't want to hear what he had to say. I didn't want this conversation to happen at all. Not with him.

"Back up," I said after a moment. "I need some space."

But he didn't move. Instead, he reached forward and grabbed my hand, holding it with both of his. "We would be unstoppable, Jade. If you help me here in Fearford, I can guarantee you get back to your sister. You would both be safe."

My breath came out in shallow pants. My vision became narrow, and everything around me suddenly didn't feel real at all. I didn't trust Isaiah. I didn't like him one bit.

But why was he saying this? Why now?

Malachi's voice booming from the distance snapped me out of my trance. "You two look cozy," he said as he approached. "I hate to break up your party, but I believe Jade told you to back up."

Isaiah dropped my hand and obeyed Malachi. I took a long, deep breath of the cool night air and leaned my head on the wall behind me. My legs shook under the weight of my body.

"We were just talking," Isaiah protested.

"You're done now," he growled. "Go home, Isaiah." Isaiah might not have noticed the way Malachi's fists were clenched tightly at his sides, but I did. I also noticed the tightness of his jaw that indicated he wasn't just mad.

He was absolutely outraged.

"Just go," I added, desperate to prevent whatever confrontation was about to happen. "We'll talk tomorrow."

Isaiah's face lit up at my words, but he didn't say anything else. Just bowed his head in my direction, then Malachi's, and stormed off toward his quarters.

But Malachi didn't come any closer. Didn't try to argue. Didn't yell. He just stood at a distance and crossed his arms over his chest, shaking his head at the ground.

"I came to make sure you were alright," he mumbled without looking at me.

I sighed, and suddenly felt the need to fight back tears. "Well, I'm not," I answered. The crack in my voice must have made Malachi look at me. "And I haven't been for a while. But thank you for checking," I answered.

My eyes burned. Malachi uncrossed his arms and stepped closer. "Jade–"

"Don't," I insisted. "Don't try to apologize."

"Fine," he said, taking another step toward me. "I won't apologize."

I couldn't hold the tears back any longer. My throat was on fire, and the hot tears spilled from my eyes. I was so damned tired. I didn't want to talk about Isaiah. I didn't want to talk about the bullshit he just spilled. I didn't want to talk about Tessa or Esther.

"I know this arrangement isn't what you wanted," he said. He took another step toward me and held my face with both his hands, using his thumb to wipe my tears. "And when this is all over, when we no longer have to fear for our lives because of my idiotic father, I'll do everything I can to make you happy, Jade. Even if that means letting you go."

It wasn't an apology. It was everything that I had been feeling between us put into words.

A harsh sob escaped my body, and my legs would have given out beneath me if it weren't for his strong arms wrapping around my waist, holding me to his chest.

"I just don't want to do this anymore," I managed to say.

"I know, princess," he whispered into my hair. "I know you don't."

Any other day I would have been pissed at the nickname, but not today. Not now.

"Will you take me somewhere?" I asked him. "Just

for a while? Somewhere we can forget about this disaster."

I heard the smile in his voice when he answered, "I thought you'd never ask."

Malachi scooped me into his arms and jumped into the air. My stomach dropped, but I buried my face into his neck as he carried us through the night.

"Won't people see us?" I asked.

"You forget that my wings are as black as the night," he laughed. "Nobody will see a thing."

"I think you scared everyone here enough already," I added.

Malachi let us drop a few feet in the air, causing me to tighten my grip on his shirt. "Saints!" I yelled. "Don't do that!"

He only laughed. "What?" he teased. "You don't like it?"

"Let's just land in one piece, thank you," I replied.

After a few minutes of flying in the darkness, Malachi obliged. He returned us to the ground in one smooth motion.

We were still in a field outside of the forest. Tall grass surrounded us, just short enough that I could barely see over it. Malachi beat his wings a few times, causing the grass around us to scatter so we had enough room.

"How about this for an escape?" he asked.

I sat down in the grass, extending my legs out in front of me. "It beats Fearford, that's certain."

"Oh, come on," he said. "It's not that bad here."

"I preferred being in danger in Rewyth. At least there I *knew* who my enemies were."

Malachi settled in the field next to me.

"This will all be over soon," he said. His tone had darkened in a way I couldn't explain. "All of it."

"Did Esther care to explain why she thought she could use your brother's blood as a sacrifice?"

"We didn't exactly get to that, no," he replied. "But at this point, that's the least of my problems."

I shook my head. "Do you think we can trust what she says about this prophecy?"

Malachi looked up at the sky. "I don't know. But I have a feeling this isn't the last we're going to hear about it."

I let my body lay back onto the field, staring up at the sky. Stars littered the black, endless void above us.

"Do you ever wonder what it would be like to just... leave? To escape and run away and never return?" I whispered.

Malachi took a long breath, but eventually reclined himself so he was lying next to me. "Sleep, Jade," is all he said. "You're safe with me."

It wasn't an answer. Saints, it wasn't even close. But it was exactly what I needed at the time. My eyelids were heavy, fighting to stay open with every blink.

I listened to the sound of Malachi's breath, steady and slow, until my eyes fluttered closed, and I drifted into that dark abyss.

CHAPTER 10
Malachi

"Saints," a man's voice jolted me awake. Jade woke at the same time, scrambling away from me on the grassy ground. The sun was rising quickly in the distance.

I jumped up, ready to confront our visitor, but it was only Serefin and the human girl. Sadie, I think her name was.

"We've been looking for you two everywhere," he continued. Sadie had her hands on her hips, a very annoyed look on her face.

"What's going on?" I asked. Jade brushed her clothes off behind me.

"Messengers came from Trithen. They're demanding to speak with the Prince of Shadows and his human bride."

My blood ran cold.

Hearing anything from Trithen was bad news.

Messengers that came just for Jade and I? Serefin gave me a look that told me he knew what I was thinking.

"Trithen?" Jade asked. "As in Rewyth's enemy kingdom?"

"One of them, yes," I answered. Rewyth didn't have a great reputation amongst the other fae kingdoms, but Trithen and Rewyth had gone to war on more than one occasion in the past few centuries.

War was never forgotten.

"Let's go," I insisted. "How in the Saints did you find us here, anyway?" I asked.

Serefin smirked. "It wasn't hard to guess, brother," he answered. Jade blushed and mumbled something under her breath, but it didn't stop me from picking her up again and launching the two of us into the air. Serefin followed with Sadie behind me.

"That was humiliating," she said when we got far enough from Ser and Sadie.

"Why?" I teased. "You think they had bad ideas about why we slept in the middle of nowhere all night long?"

"Saints," she mumbled. "At least it was Serefin and not one of the others."

"You can trust him, princess," I replied.

"I know I can, but what about Sadie? This can't be helping my reputation."

"Your reputation?" I asked. "As my wife, you mean?"

"Yes," she answered firmly. "Exactly."

A few moments later, I was lowering us to the ground inside the front gates of Fearford.

Esther was the first to greet us. "Where have you two been!" she yelled. "You can't just go off like that without telling anybody! We thought you..."

"Left this damned place?" I finished for her. "Not yet, but don't give us any ideas."

Jade stiffened as Esther rushed forward and hugged her.

It looked like a completely normal action for Esther, but Jade looked as if she had never been hugged before.

"Are you alright?" she asked Jade. "Are you hurt?"

"No," Jade answered. "I'm fine."

It was odd watching my mother care for someone. Part of me wondered if she worried about Jade's well-being or if this had more to do with the fact that Jade was somehow special to Esther.

Time would tell.

"Where are they?" I interrupted. "The messengers from Trithen?"

"This way," Sadie spoke, charging in front of us and leading the way. Jade, Serefin and I followed behind her.

Nobody spoke. Not as Sadie led us to an open, unoccupied wooden structure in Fearford and not as she held the door open for us to walk inside.

I had been nervous before in my lifetime.

There were countless times that my father had sent me into life-or-death situations. Did I really care? Maybe not. But those situations were the same ones that made your palms sweaty. That made you double count your breath before you walked inside.

Those were the situations that made you feel alive, also.

"There you are," a voice greeted us as we walked through the door. "It's about time," it continued.

My eyes adjusted to the dim light of the room, and I waited until I felt Serefin and Jade's presence behind me before I answered, "What do you want?"

"Is that how you welcome all your guests to your new kingdom, Malachi Weyland?" the man asked.

I bit my tongue. "Who are you and why are you here?" I asked. "Who sent you?"

"Easy now," one of the messengers said. His slicked back, blonde hair was annoying enough. His boots had been freshly cleaned, and there wasn't a flaw to be seen on his uniform.

Total prick.

"We heard the infamous Prince of Shadows had taken up residence in one of the human colonies. We just came to see if it was true or not, that's all."

"You're lying," I answered. Jade stood still as stone behind me.

"You're right," the other messenger said. "We are lying. Our king sent us to find out what was really going on here. Fae taking over human lands is prohibited. We could have the Paragon here within days."

My anger flared, and it took everything in me to keep my temper cool enough so that my power didn't lose control. Of course they came here to rat on us to the Paragon. I'm sure the first thing my father did was tell everyone that fae were taking over Fearford.

It was his insurance policy.

Unless Trithen wanted something else from us.

My mind spun, trying to find anything to say to the bastards.

Jade took her chance and spoke up next. "That won't be necessary," she said. "The fae aren't taking over anything here. They're breaking no treaty. Fearford has welcomed them here as guests."

"Is that so?" the blonde one asked. "And who is this pretty lady?"

Jade opened her mouth to answer but I cut her off. I didn't need these strangers knowing who my wife was. "That's none of your concern," I growled. "You're speaking to me."

Serefin stepped forward next. "Did you come all this way to threaten the heir to the fae throne, gentleman?"

I choked back a smile. Serefin always had a respectful tone, but there was also an edge to him that surprised even me from time to time.

Blondie's friend stepped forward. "Look," he said. "Our king heard there were fae living here. We also heard the Prince of Shadows hasn't been seen in Rewyth for a bit of time now. We took a wild guess, and now we see that it's true. But we didn't just come here to verify our suspicions."

"Oh really?" I taunted.

He rolled his eyes but continued. "We come with

an invitation. Bring yourselves to Trithen to speak with our king in person, and we won't report whatever the Saints is happening here to the Paragon."

My fists clenched. The air around me shook, barely noticeable. "Calm down," Jade whispered. It didn't work.

"You have one week. Bring the humans, too. Our king wants to know how much of this arrangement is mutually beneficial." And as quickly as those Trithen bastards appeared here, they were gone.

"I'm going to find Isaiah," Sadie said before she rushed out the door.

I couldn't move. I couldn't think. I had yet to process what just happened.

"The Paragon can't actually punish you for this, can they? You're only here because your father ordered you to come." Serefin asked.

I shook my head. Yes, my father had ordered me to come here. But that wasn't the whole story.

Trithen knew very little about what had happened the last few weeks, if anything at all. Unless they had spies in Rewyth, which wouldn't exactly be surprising to anybody.

"What does that mean?" Jade whispered to me. "That they'll report you?"

"The fae have plenty of rules we have to follow, although it may not always seem like it," I replied. "The Paragon is a group of powerful fae and witches both. They draw the line. Centuries ago, they drew up a few treaties. Basically commands that we have to live by to keep us in line. It's vague stuff, really, and they usually don't bother following through with any punishments, anyway. But the threat is still there."

"Why?" she asked. "For just being here? For just living with humans for a few days?"

"I guess so," I replied. "There's an old treaty stating that the fae cannot invade human lands. Fearford is a human territory, and, well, here we are."

"But they don't mind that you're married to a human? Wouldn't that break some sort of treaty that you have?"

I shrugged. "Yes and no. But like I said, they usually don't care what we do either way. It's rare for them to show up in any of our business. I haven't heard from the Paragon in a decade or two."

She shook her head, as if she were just letting the weight of the situation hit her.

"But if they do come for you..." she started.

"Don't worry," Serefin interrupted. "Mal isn't doing anything wrong. Trithen is just blowing their horns at this point. They have no pull with the Paragon, it's all a bluff."

Jade nodded and took a deep breath. "What makes them so powerful?" she asked. "Why is everyone afraid of them?"

I exchanged a glance with Ser.

"Hey," Jade interrupted. "I know that look. You guys have to tell me. I'll find out eventually, you know I will."

It's not like I wanted to hide things from Jade. She

had learned a lot today, and she had enough problems to deal with between my mother and this crazy prophecy she insisted Jade was part of.

The truth was, the Paragon and I didn't always have a great relationship. Yes, it had been decades since I had heard from them. But it felt like a calm before chaos. The Paragon had never been out of my life for that long. They had always been right around the corner, watching my every move.

Waiting for me to make a mistake.

Saints. Maybe today was that day.

"Some of them have powers like Mal," Ser answered slowly. "The witches are powerful, more powerful than Esther. The fae are ruthless. They possess gifts some people have only heard about in stories. They'll enforce any rule they wish to on anyone they see fit. There's simply no match to their power. That's why they are feared."

Jade nodded. I relaxed a small amount.

"You're not telling me something," she said after a second.

This damned girl.

"They were impressed by my *special* gifts when they learned of them. Let's just leave it at that," I said.

Jade's eyes lit up. "Really? What did they want from you?"

"The same thing everyone wants, princess. Power. They see my gift as a threat and they want to use it for themselves."

It was easy to talk about now, but that hadn't always been the case.

"Fine," Jade said after a few seconds, taking the hint. "What do we do about it? Go there and walk into an ambush?"

Jade didn't know what I knew about Trithen.

Serefin caught my eye but I shook my head, just enough for him to see. Nobody else would find out what we knew.

"There won't be an ambush," I said. "But if they're true about reporting to the Paragon, it's in our best interest to not call their bluff."

Jade nodded, although I could tell from the look she gave me that she would be asking me about this later.

Sadie and Isaiah broke into the room, Isaiah was out of breath. "What did I miss?" he asked.

"Pack your bag, champ," I said. "We're being summoned to Trithen."

"Trithen as in the largest fae territory?" he asked.

"That's arguable," Serefin chimed in. "Largest behind Rewyth, of course."

"Right," Isaiah said. "That one."

"We don't really have a choice," I added. "Your presence was requested, too."

"You didn't think to tell me when messengers arrived? Isn't that something I should know?"

"They weren't exactly waiting around for you," I said. "And nothing you would have done would have stopped them."

"This is my kingdom," Isaiah spat. "If fae are trespassing, I need to know about it."

"Why?" Jade asked him. Her tone was purely inquisitive, but the way she crossed her arms over her chest was dominant.

I didn't try to hide my smile.

Isaiah looked at her like it was the first time he had ever laid eyes on her. "Why?" he repeated. "Why would I want to know about two fae breaking the treaty?"

"What would you do about it?" she asked. "Stop them?"

Isaiah clenched his fists. I could have predicted each of his next moves down to the second. I had seen it hundreds of times. He was a young man fighting for power where he had none.

"Don't pretend like you're in charge here, Isaiah," I said calmly. "Our presence is being requested in Trithen, and we're going."

"Sounds like you're not in charge here either, then, *Prince of Shadows*."

"Unless we all want to die, we'll go," I said. My words were harsh enough to be final.

And they were true. If it was true that the Paragon was going to be involved, we had to comply.

Where the Paragon was involved, death was always close by.

CHAPTER 11
Jade

I hadn't heard the word *Paragon* at all in my nearly eighteen years of life until I had moved to Rewyth.

Now, however, the word alone shook me to my core.

The Paragon were the ultimate punishers of the fae. Sure, there were different fae kingdoms. But they each answered to the Paragon.

And with Rewyth being the most powerful fae kingdom, they had a special eye on the Prince of Shadows.

My husband.

Adeline had taken the time to explain to me that the Paragon didn't mind when a fae married a human as long as the human went willingly, or there was a deal agreed on by both parties.

Until now, they weren't doing anything wrong.

But with Malachi and the others staying in Fearford, it caused some problems.

This was all speculation, of course. Those messengers from Trithen could have been making it all up just to get us to do what they wanted.

We couldn't risk not believing them.

"Are you ready for this?" Adeline asked. She had joined me with Sadie to prepare for our trip. Sadie didn't have much, but compared to what we had brought to Fearford, she had everything. She let Adeline and I both borrow a spare change of clothes, consisting of simple trousers and a light jacket.

It was hot enough to sweat through multiple layers, but Adeline insisted we would need protection where we were going.

We didn't argue.

"Am I allowed to say no?" I asked. Adeline finished zipping her backpack. She had a long, tight braid that flowed down her back.

"It won't be anything to worry about," she replied. "Just politics. This type of thing happens all the time."

"Really?" Sadie interrupted. "Other fae really threaten to report you to this Paragon thing frequently?"

Adeline hesitated. "Well–"

"Right," Sadie replied. "That's what I thought."

Sadie and Adeline were complete opposites. Adeline was tall, classy and elegant. Sadie had short, dark hair and had an arm full of tattoos.

Still. I think Adeline was happy to have the company.

Sadie on the other hand...

"You've never left Fearford?" I asked her, attempting to change the conversation.

"Never had to. This place has provided for us enough, although you all might not think so."

"I didn't choose to come here, Sadie. Neither did Adeline," I said. Adeline didn't need my backup, but I somehow felt the need to defend her.

Sadie exhaled a long breath before flinging her own bag over her shoulder. "I know. This is just all very different, and I can't say anything good has happened since fae showed up in Fearford."

Adeline raised an eyebrow.

"Yeah," I admitted. "I have a feeling that streak will only continue."

"They're probably waiting for us," Adeline said. "We should probably get going."

She trotted out the door, leaving Sadie and I behind.

"You can stay here, you know. The fae in Trithen would never know," I said.

Sadie shook her head. "If Isaiah's going, I'm going. He'll never make it without me. Besides, I'd like a chance to get outside these walls. As comfortable as they may be."

That I understood.

"So, you and Isaiah..." I led on.

Sadie quickly shut it down. "Never. You know how

it is. He likes to pretend to be in charge, to call all the shots. But at the end of the day, when he needs advice, it's me he comes running to. That's how it's always been. I've known the guy my whole life."

"You're a good friend to him," I admitted.

Sadie smiled. It made me think that I hadn't seen her smile like that much at all.

She wasn't as tough of a badass as she looked.

"Let's go," she said, pink rushing to her cheeks. "We're going to be late."

I couldn't help but smile as I followed Sadie out of her room.

The sun was beating down. I squinted my eyes and immediately wished I could cut off half of my hair. It was longer now, hitting almost to my waist. Adeline had twisted it into a braid similar to hers, but the thickness of it still sat heavy on my neck.

"You princesses ready to go?" Lucien yelled from across the clearing. "We've been waiting all morning."

"Don't call me that," we replied in unison.

That earned a laugh from us both.

"Ignore him," I whispered to her. "He's terrible and crude and has no redeeming qualities."

"And any of the fae do?" she replied.

Now it was my turn to blush. "You'll see," was all I could manage to say.

The group of us looked like we were prepared for a six month adventure. Isaiah and Sadie were the two humans joining the group, other than myself. Then we had the fae, which included Malachi, Adeline of course, and the brothers– Adonis, Lucien, and the twins. Serefin refused to stay here while Malachi went, so he was tagging along, too.

And then there was Esther.

Nobody wanted her to come. Saints. I have no idea why *she* even wanted to come. Her relationship with Malachi's brothers freaked me out. It was weird, to say the least. They had all sworn a blood oath to her and nobody seemed to want to talk about that, or why they would do something like that in the first place.

But I wasn't about to start asking questions. I knew Malachi was thinking all of the same things. And she was his mother, after all.

"Horses?" I asked. "We aren't just flying there?"

Malachi laughed. "As much as we would love to carry you humans across an entire kingdom, this is the safest option."

I nodded, remembering what he had said about some fae being stronger flyers than others.

"Fine," I replied. "But I get my own horse."

And I regretted those words as soon as I said them.

There weren't enough horses for all of us.

And Malachi was technically my husband, which meant they probably expected us to ride together.

Malachi knew it, too. He leaned against the massive white stallion with his arms crossed over his chest, a smirk on his mouth as he chewed on a small twig.

"Don't look at me like that," I said to him as I passed him, shoving his shoulder with my own.

"Like what?" he replied. "This is my normal look."

"No," I responded. "It's not. Your normal look is the one where everyone you talk to thinks you're about to kill them."

"And you're saying this isn't that look?" he said, smiling again.

I rolled my eyes.

A bead of sweat was already forming at my temple.

"How long of a trip is this, anyway?" I asked.

"It will only take two days if we keep moving," Adonis replied.

"Three days is more reasonable," Isaiah chimed in.

"Yeah?" Lucien sneered. "And how would you know? Have you been to Trithen before?"

Isaiah's jaw tightened. The obvious answer was no.

"No fighting, please," Esther yelled from her own horse. "We have plenty of time for that on the road."

That seemed to shut everyone up.

We spent the next few minutes packing the bags onto the horses. Isaiah and Sadie spent their time digging through maps and planning a clear route.

But the fae did no such thing.

"Are you not the least bit concerned that we'll get lost out there?" I asked.

"Why?" Malachi answered as he finished feeding the white stallion a large apple. "Are you?"

"You know what I mean," I said. "Just answer the question."

He took a deep breath before answering, "It's a straight shot, princess. Getting lost isn't the thing we need to worry about out there."

Serefin walked up next to him.

My blood ran cold.

"You don't mean..."

"More deadlings?" Sereifn answered for me. "You bet. And we'll get lucky if that's all we'll see."

Saints. How stupid was I to assume that the dangers in the woods were only between Rewyth and the walls to my own human lands? Of course they would be everywhere. There was a reason these walls existed.

"Do they know?" I asked, pointing to Isaiah and Sadie.

Mal shrugged, and gave Serefin a knowing look. "They'll find out soon enough. No need to scare them."

I sighed and wiped the sweat from my forehead with the back of my hand. I couldn't believe I agreed with that. We could be walking into a death trap, and yet...

Trithen could be a death trap of its own. Isaiah and Sadie knew the risks.

And here they were.

"Fine," I said. "But any weird, mythical creature tries to attack me, I'm throwing you between us," I said to Malachi. "And I mean it."

Malachi just laughed. "I would be disappointed if you didn't."

He locked eyes on me, and his expression alone made my stomach flip. Serefin left to get settled on his own horse, following the rest of the group as they exited through the narrow entryway of Fearford's walls.

Malachi held out his hand. "Your turn, princess."

"I can get on a horse by myself, thank you," I replied.

"Really?" he teased. "That's not how I remembered it last time."

"I wasn't in riding condition last time, was I?" I asked. A flash of emotion crossed his features, but I ignored it. The last time Malachi had seen me attempt getting on a horse, I had just been whipped by his father's men. The memory was fresh in my mind, and I could imagine it was even fresher in Malachi's.

"I'll kill them, you know," he whispered as I turned to get on the saddle. He picked up a loose strand of my hair that had fallen out of my braid. "I'll kill them for what they did to you that day."

He didn't have to say it. I knew he would get his vengeance one day.

"I know," I whispered back.

We stayed there for a moment, looking at each other in the blazing heat of the sun.

Until Malachi cleared his throat and turned to help me on the saddle.

"Alright," he said. "Jump on and move forward."

I did what I was told, grateful that the heat covered the blood rushing to my face.

My body rested easily on the saddle, much different from the last time I had ridden. Malachi was behind me within a second, effortlessly throwing himself onto the back of the horse.

"You sure you don't want to fly?" I asked him. His arms settled around mine as he grabbed the reins.

"Why?" he asked, his breath against my ear sent a chill down my spine. "Are you afraid?"

I rolled my eyes, but the edge in his voice sent a warmth through my body.

Malachi laughed behind me, sending vibrations through my back. I kept my spine stiff, but Malachi was clearly making no effort to keep his distance on the saddle. His legs tapped against mine with every step the massive horse took, and his chest pressed tightly against my back as we moved into a steady walk at the back of the group.

"Just like old times," he whispered. "Let's hope this trip goes differently than that one."

"At least we don't have to worry about your brothers killing me this time."

"That's true," he agreed. "But I wouldn't be so trusting of the group."

My interest peaked. "Why?" I asked. "You don't trust them?"

He took a deep breath. "I don't trust anyone so easily, princess. Neither should you. Keep your guard up, even with Sadie. We don't know what they really want."

"And your mother?"

"Her too."

I nodded, and Malachi and I fell into a silent trot

for hours. His body against mine became more and more comfortable as the journey continued. He didn't make any annoying comments as I let my body relax into his, leaning on him for support.

The forest was beautiful. With the sun blazing down, it was easy to see all the different life out here. It wasn't terrifying and disastrous. It was peaceful, with a certain darkness that would lure you in if you weren't too careful.

It felt familiar.

Massive trees towered around us, and they became thicker and thicker as we advanced forward. Humidity increased, too. Within the next hour, nearly my entire shirt had been soaked with sweat.

"You'd be a lot cooler if you just took that off, you know," Malachi whispered in my ear when he saw me fidgeting. I elbowed him in the ribs.

"Ow!" he exclaimed. "I was just trying to help!"

I was about to come up with any insult I could think of when Isaiah stopped at the front of the group.

"There's water here," he said. "Let's stop for a break."

Nobody objected, and the group of us brought our horses around a small clearing near the river we had been following through the forest.

Sweat covered every inch of my skin. Malachi's, too, as he swung himself off the horse. He reached up and grabbed my waist to help me down, his fingers brushing under my shirt and sliding against my skin.

"Thanks," I mumbled before quickly straightening and turning to the others.

It's not that I was embarrassed to show affection. I wasn't. I had just never shown affection publicly before. And Malachi was *complicated*.

Nobody seemed to be paying us any attention, though. Everyone tied their horses to a nearby tree and gathered around the water.

I knelt on the ground, dipping my hands into the stream. It was cool water, covered by the shade of the massive trees. I cupped my hands and threw water over my face, letting it drip down my neck. I threw another handful on my back.

We all looked ridiculous, as if we had already been riding for days.

This was definitely going to be a long trip.

Esther knelt next to me, mimicking my movements. "It's amazing, isn't it?" she asked.

"What is?"

"That the forest gives us what we need." She cupped her hands and took a long drink of the river water.

"Yeah," I suggested. Even though Esther had a strange way of talking. "I guess so."

"How are you feeling, girl?" she asked.

"Fine."

She eyed me suspiciously, as if she didn't fully believe my answer. "That will change, you know," she said.

"What?" I asked. "What will change?"

"How you're feeling. Things are going to start changing for you very soon."

"What do you mean? I'm going to get sick?"

She took a moment before responding, "Not sick, child. Just different. You and I have a lot to discuss."

Now it was my turn to eye her. I hadn't noticed before, but her long, silver hair was littered with small beads and gems. She definitely looked older, yet her skin had an olive glow that radiated youth.

Esther hadn't been explicitly rude to me, she was just strange.

And after Malachi told me what she had been planning for me...

"What do you plan to do when we return from Trithen?" I asked her in a hushed voice that only she could hear.

"What I've always done," she responded.

"And what is that? What does the mother of the fae heir do while she hides from everyone she abandoned?"

The sudden wave of emotion surprised me, but Esther didn't look the slightest bit troubled. "I know you think I am cruel. For leaving Malachi."

"I don't think much of anything about you, actually," I responded.

"But you'll get to know me more I hope. I would like it very much if you and I were friends."

"Why?" I asked. "Because you need something from me?"

"No, I am trying to help you, Jade."

My name felt *powerful* when she said it. It sounded strong.

Something inside of me stirred.

"You *are* a witch, aren't you?" I asked, hoping she would confirm the rumors.

"Something like that, yes."

"So that makes Malachi only half fae?" I whispered.

Esther released a long breath, eyeing the water instead of holding eye contact with me. "That is a very long story, Jade. A story for another time, maybe."

I got the feeling it was a story we would need to know sooner rather than later, but I let the subject go.

Next to us, Isaiah peeled his shirt off and jumped into the water, splashing everyone. Sadie let out a squeal when he shoved a wave of water into her face.

"What!" he exclaimed. "It feels amazing! You all should give it a shot!"

"No thanks," Adeline responded. "You have no clue what you're swimming with in there. It could be nasty!"

"Or dangerous," Adonis added.

I glanced at him and quickly looked away. The less time I spent talking with Malachi's brothers, the better.

"What about you, Jade? Care to join me for a swim?"

Malachi snorted a laugh behind me, but turned and followed his brothers and Adeline back to our camp.

It was so incredibly hot, and the cool water felt amazing on my skin.

"You know what?" I replied, standing from my knelt position by the river. "A swim sounds great."

Isaiah looked at me in shock as I kicked my boots off and jumped in, fully clothed.

The water was deeper than I expected. I sank a few feet before kicking my legs, sending my body toward the blue surface.

The current was soft, gently trickling around my body.

Isaiah roared in laughter as I broke through the surface. "Wow, I really didn't think you had that in you," he said.

"You think I'm some sort of Saint?" I asked.

Isaiah splashed a handful of water in my direction. "Hey!" I yelled.

"What?" he teased. "Afraid of water now?"

He splashed again, but I didn't flinch away this time. Instead, dipped my head under water, swam toward him, and yanked him underneath with me.

I almost choked on my own laughter as we both surfaced, Isaiah gasping for air.

"Oh, you really want to play that game?" he teased. I laughed again and moved to swim away, but Isaiah's arms caught me and yanked me under again before I could get out of reach.

He let go quickly, and we both resurfaced seconds later. "Okay!" I yelled, out of breath from the water and the laughter. "Okay, we're even now!"

Isaiah looked different. He wasn't the annoying, broody leader of Fearford. He was just a boy. A young one at that. I caught myself wondering how I would act if I had an entire kingdom in my hands. If my father had died, leaving me with all that responsibility at such a young age.

"You're staring," he interrupted.

I blushed and quickly looked away. "Sorry," I admitted. "I just have a hard time believing you really run an entire kingdom."

"What?" he asked. "Is that so hard to believe?"

"Yes," I responded. "You're barely older than me. What are you, twenty?"

"I will be in a couple of weeks," he said.

Saints. He was even younger than I thought.

"What about you?" he asked. "You have to be what, eighteen? Nineteen?"

"I'll be turning eighteen in a couple of days, actually," I replied. "Although I definitely feel much older than that."

"Being married so young can't help."

We both tread the water around us, relaxing in the cool stream of water.

"Trust me, I've lived through much worse than being married off."

"Really? Even to the fae prince?"

"He's not as bad as you think. He keeps me safe. That's more than I can say for any human back home."

"So, you plan on staying with him, then? You actually *like* being his wife?"

I couldn't ignore the tiny hint of disdain in his voice. The small amount of envy. "I don't know," I said.

"I don't know what I'm doing anymore. I couldn't make it back home if I tried. Rewyth isn't my home, not so long as the King is alive."

"What about Fearford?" he asked. "Would Fearford ever be an option for you?"

His question caught me off guard. My mind went completely blank, but it didn't matter anyway because small hands wrapped around both of my ankles.

Isaiah was close, but not that close.

I kicked twice, but the grips on my ankles didn't move. "What is that?" I asked Isaiah. I splashed around frantically, trying but failing to see what had taken hold of me in the water. "Isaiah?"

"What? What is it?"

"I don't know, something's–"

I was pulled under before I could get the words out.

CHAPTER 12
Jade

My lungs tightened immediately as I was plunged deeper and deeper into the water. I kicked and thrashed, but the grip on my ankles only tightened.

Someone was trying to drown me. Someone or something.

I felt someone reaching for me, I desperately grabbed onto anything I could. Isaiah. Isaiah would help me.

The water wasn't that deep, I just had to reach the surface.

He was trying to pull me up, but whatever was holding me to the bottom of the river wasn't going to budge. The grip on me was so tight, sharp pain began shooting up my legs.

I was going to die here. If this thing didn't let go of me, I was going to drown.

I let go of Isaiah and reached down, trying to pry the grip off of myself. But it was no use.

I clawed and clawed and *clawed* at the hands, at the deadly grip that wouldn't let up.

There were many times in my life that I had accepted death. Saints, there were even times that I would have welcomed it.

But this was not one of those times.

Desperation controlled my movements. Isaiah's hands found mine once again, and he pulled so hard I thought my shoulders were going to pop.

People were yelling above me, but I could only hear the muffled noises from below the water.

My lungs screamed. I was three seconds away from inhaling a mouthful of water.

Two seconds.

One second.

The water around me stilled, and the grip on my legs let go. I didn't hesitate. I kicked toward the surface, Isaiah's hands pulling me toward the air.

The next few moments were a blur of coughing, choking up water, and being dragged out of the water by both Esther and Isaiah.

The others rushed toward us, but Malachi was the only one I saw as he dropped to his knees in front of me, peeling me away from Isaiah.

"What happened?" he yelled, possessive anger booming in his voice.

"I scared them off, but nobody's getting back in

that damn water," Esther replied. "It was a kraken. It had to be."

"It was strong," Isaiah added. "If it weren't for Esther she would have drowned."

"Keep your hands off my wife," Malachi growled in his direction. "Jade," he whispered to me. "Jade, are you okay?"

I coughed one more time and pushed my wet hair out of my face. "Yeah, I'm fine," I answered.

I pulled myself into a sitting position, my wet clothes dragging me down. The group had backed up, giving Malachi and I some space as I recovered.

"I'm fine," I repeated, more for myself. "That thing was going to kill me," I said, shaking my head.

"I wouldn't have let that happen," Malachi replied.

"Wait a minute," Isaiah interrupted. "You're telling me that thing was a kraken? As in, the sea monster kraken?"

"Yes," Esther replied. "Don't be so quick to dismiss the stories of your elders, son."

"Let's give them some space," Adeline said. "Dinner isn't going to cook itself."

I gave her a half-hearted smile when she winked at me, and after a few minutes Mal and I sat alone on the riverbank.

His eyebrows were furrowed, and his jaw was clenched.

I knew that look.

"What?" I asked him. "What's wrong?"

He didn't look at me. Didn't respond. I followed

his gaze to see what he was staring at in the distance with such a death glare.

Isaiah.

"Calm down," I said. "He's harmless!"

I even surprised myself with saying those words. Isaiah was harmless for now. Away from Fearford and the mess of politics that he was trying to put on a show for, he was just a regular guy.

Mal had nothing to fear.

"Still," Malachi responded. "Something's off."

I shook my head. "Whatever you say, Mal. He was trying to save me."

"The sun will be setting soon. Your clothes are wet," he said, changing the conversation.

"Great observation. Would you rather me have jumped in naked?"

"Isaiah would have preferred that, I'm sure."

"Come on!" I exclaimed. I stepped closer to Malachi and mimicked his body language, crossing my arms over my chest just inches from him. "All he did was pull me out of the water. Are you jealous, Malachi Weyland?"

He finally took his gaze off Isaiah and looked me in the eye. His stare was intense enough to send a chill down my spine.

"You don't want to see me jealous, princess."

"And why is that?"

He smirked for a moment before answering, "Because some people tell me I have quite the temper."

"Is that so?" I asked.

"Mhmm."

"Better keep my distance then," I teased, before turning around and walking back to the group of horses. Adeline appeared back in the clearing, followed by Serefin, carrying an armful of wood and sticks.

"For a fire?" I asked. "Isn't it a little hot for that?"

"It's going to get a lot cooler around here once the sun goes down," Adeline responded. "You'll be happy you took that jacket along with you."

We spent the next few hours eating some of the food we brought with us, feeding the horses, and trying not to rip each other's heads off.

Correction—the *brothers* tried not to rip each other's heads off.

It amazed me that they still bickered this much, that there was still so much tension between them all. The brothers had kidnapped me and put my life in danger, but it was all to protect me.

Allegedly.

I could see why Malachi wasn't so quick to accept their friendship. Adonis was really the only one who was trying, anyway. The others seemed like they couldn't care less.

Although I did catch them whispering amongst themselves and turning to look at Malachi on a number of occasions.

Something was up.

"Are they always like this?" Sadie whispered to me. The sun was starting to go down, and as the temperature dropped with it, we all had gravitated around the fire.

"For the short time that I've known them, yes," I answered. "It can get exhausting."

"Why does Malachi hate them so much?" she asked. "They're brothers, aren't they?"

"Half-brothers," Esther chimed in. "Malachi is my only son. The others are sons of the new Queen."

"Oh," Sadie stuttered. "I didn't realize. I'm sorry."

"Don't be," Esther continued. "The King doesn't discuss my time in Rewyth much at all. It's easier if everyone assumes Malachi is their true brother."

"That's why he's the heir to the throne?" Sadie asked. "Because he's your only son?"

Esther nodded. "My blood runs deep in Rewyth. I may not be there now, but Malachi will one day carry on my legacy. As soon as that bastard is off the throne."

"Wow," I chimed in. "You seem to have strong feelings about the King."

Esther gave me a knowing look. "Same as you, child. Same as you."

"What made you leave?" Sadie asked. I stiffened, knowing this answer would not be short and Sadie was brave to ask it in the first place.

Esther just smiled. "There were many things that led to my departure," she started. "But there are things that you two don't know yet. Things I'm sure your prince wouldn't appreciate me sharing."

I glanced at Malachi, who was too busy bickering with Eli and Fynn to pay any attention to us.

"Like what?"

Esther glanced at them, also, making sure there were no lingering ears on us.

"There has been talk of a new world. A world where fae and humans can get along in peace."

"What do you mean? Don't we get along just fine now?"

"With separation, yes," Esther continued. "I'm talking about together. In the same kingdom. No human kingdoms and fae kingdoms, just kingdoms."

"Really?" I asked, my interest piqued. "And I somehow have something to do with that?"

"As I said before, child, if everything we know is correct, you are the peacemaker. You are the key to everything."

Amazement, surprise, and curiosity all ran through me. "Those are just stories, though," Sadie said. "How can you be sure Jade is the one?"

Esther looked at me now, and with the reflection of the fire in her eyes, I saw genuine love. Genuine caring. She lifted a loose strand of my now partially-dried hair and placed it behind my ear. "I just know, child. I just know."

"That's why you saved my life," I said. "You had been waiting on me?"

Esther nodded.

I looked down at my boots. "It can't be me, though. I'm just a human. There's nothing special about me."

"And that, child, is where you are so painfully wrong."

I wanted to ask her a million questions. I wanted her to explain everything to me, about who she was and where she came from. I wanted to hear her talk about Malachi and what life was like before she left Rewyth. I wanted to know what she thought of the King and how she felt about leaving Malachi all this time.

What had she been doing? Why had she never tried to reach out to him? To protect him?

"What are we talking about over here?" Isaiah interrupted as he sat on the ground next to us. Esther stiffened but smiled at Isaiah.

"Just girl things," she lied. Interesting. Esther was keeping this hidden from Isaiah? I wondered if Sadie would do the same. "It would bore you."

"Anything is less boring than listening to them fight about nothing," he added. Sadie smiled at him, but still said nothing.

I decided to change the conversation. "So, Isaiah," I asked. "What are your plans for Fearford when we return?"

Isaiah nodded, clearly appreciating that some attention was now on him. "I have many plans for Fearford, Jade. As you know, humans have always lived in poverty. Humans have suffered for decades–if not centuries."

"Trust me, I know," I said.

"I want that to change. My father wanted that, too. But he never had the means to fulfill that."

"How could you possibly fulfill that?" I asked.

Isaiah held his hands out, gesturing to the fae on the other side of the fire and to us on this side of the fire. "We work together," he said.

Sadie laughed out loud.

"It sounds ridiculous, yes," he said. "But it's already starting. The fact that we're even taking this journey together is a step in the right direction."

I admired his thinking, I really did. But after living in Rewyth for a short amount of time, I knew it was a flawed plan. The fae were greedy. They loved their expensive things and their fancy parties.

They loved power.

They loved being powerful.

And they weren't going to give that up for a human. Not now, not ever. Isaiah was surely not the first person with a plan like this.

The King had thought of it, yes. But only to advance his own goal of getting the fae closer to enemy territory.

And that was clearly working so well.

But men like Isaiah, just like fae men, wanted power. The only difference was that Isaiah had none.

The fae held all the power.

"Let's get some sleep," Esther suggested. "It won't be long until we're on the road again."

We agreed, and everyone moved to get their sleeping bags from the back of the horses.

As soon as I stepped away from the fire, the cool of the night hit me. I wrapped my arms around myself but it was no help. My clothes were mostly dry, but not dry enough to hold onto any body heat.

Saints. It had to have dropped at least twenty degrees in the last half hour.

"Regretting that swim yet?" Malachi snuck up on me.

"Not at all," I lied. "Why do you ask?"

Malachi laughed and shook his head. "You know if you want to borrow my blanket, you can just ask."

"I'm fine," I responded back. I didn't need any favors from Malachi, not any more than he had already given me.

"If you say so, princess," he said. He reached around me, arms brushing my body on both sides as he grabbed his own blanket off the horse. "Don't say I didn't offer," he whispered in my ear.

My fists clenched. Malachi was infuriating. And now that he knew I was willing to kiss him in the middle of the crowd of humans during the bonfire, he was willing to tease me every second we were together in return.

It was torture.

I shook it off, grabbing my blanket and the extra jacket Adeline had made me pack, before walking back toward the fire.

"I'll take first watch," Adonis announced. "I'll wake you in two hours," he said to Malachi.

Malachi hesitated, but ultimately agreed. We positioned ourselves scattered around the fire, everyone making sure they could feel some heat.

I chose an empty spot and laid my blanket down on the dirt.

Malachi motioned to Serefin, who nodded and moved to settle in on my right.

Malachi did the same on my left.

"Are you serious?" I whispered to him. "I don't need babysitters."

He eyed Serefin again, who didn't budge.

"It's not you I'm worried about, Jade," he said. Any teasing in his voice was gone now, replaced with a brutal seriousness. "Just go to sleep."

Normally, I would have argued. I would have spat back some sort of comment as to how he would just boss me around like that.

But this time...

This time I listened.

The cold night easily bit through my thin blanket. Even with my jacket wrapped tightly around my body, I was freezing.

How could it possibly be this cold?

It didn't take long until the whispering from the others subsided, everyone falling fast asleep.

Except for me.

And I didn't dare ask Malachi for warmth. Not when I had already objected so vocally.

I clenched my jaw, and focused on tightening every muscle in my body every few seconds to encourage some sort of blood movement.

I flipped from side to side, letting the heat from the fire warm one side of my body, and then the other.

"Warm enough, princess?" Mal whispered in the darkness. He had gotten closer since I last checked.

Much closer.

"Yes," I responded. "Very comfortable, thank you."

Mal chuckled lightly.

I didn't have to look at what he was doing. As soon as I heard the movement of fabric, I knew.

"Good," he responded. "I would hate for you to be cold. Wouldn't want you getting sick on the first night of our journey."

I clenched my jaw. Tightened my muscles. "Nope," I said through gritted teeth. "None of that happening here."

More movement.

Malachi's arm brushed against mine. He was moving closer. "Apologies," he whispered. "You don't mind if I sleep here, do you?" he asked. His body was very close to mine now. If I were to slide an inch to the left, we would be touching.

"You can do whatever you want to do," I answered.

Malachi made a noise of satisfaction and settled into his new spot on the ground.

I tried to remain still. I tried not to shiver. But Malachi was too close now, and I was far too cold to try and hide anything.

"Saints," he mumbled under his breath before rolling sideways, pressing his body close to mine. He extended his blanket so it covered me, as well, giving me an extra layer of warmth. "Don't even try to object," he insisted. "Or else neither of us will get any sleep."

I kept my mouth shut, and instead focused on the warmth of his body that was radiating through the thick blanket.

"Thank you," I mumbled after my body finally quit shivering.

Mal chuckled silently, but I felt the vibrations through the fabric. His arm was draped over my body, but he left it at that, giving me plenty of space yet plenty of warmth.

Somehow, he still held the ability to surprise me.

"Sleep, princess," he whispered. "I'll wake you in the morning."

With my body tucked tightly next to Malachi, and Serefin fast asleep on the other side of me, I let my heavy eyelids flicker closed.

T hunder cracked across the sky, the ground in front of me illuminating with lightning for just a moment before disappearing into the darkness again.

I turned my head upward, only to be greeted by heavy raindrops slapping my skin.

Dread encapsulated me. In my bones, taking over my every waking sense.

I was paralyzed by fear, but I didn't know why. And where was I? How had I gotten here?

"Jade!" a voice yelled to me. "Jade, run!"

Run. I had to run. I had to move.

My legs were frozen, unable to get me away from something that I wasn't sure was after me...

It was so dark, so cold.

Another crack of thunder.

Another flash of light.

I took a deep breath of the thick, wet air and put all of my effort into picking up my foot. One step at a time. I had to get out. I had to escape.

From something, if not my mind.

One foot in front of the other, my bare feet sank into the mud.

"Run from what?" I yelled back after I mustered the nerve to yell back. At who? I couldn't tell.

Everything was blurry. So, so blurry.

"You won't make it!" it yelled back. But I knew that voice. I had heard that voice hundreds of times before.

Malachi.

I knew the name, but who was he to me? How did I know Malachi?

It didn't matter. What mattered was getting out. Getting away.

Running.

I ran as quickly as my feet could move, which wasn't quick at all.

Wasn't quick enough.

It was only a matter of time before whoever was chasing me caught me, and then I would be dead.

Death was always coming for me. Always.

"Malachi," I whispered. The name sounded foreign

on my mouth, but familiar to my body. "Malachi!" I repeated a little lower. "Help me!" I yelled to him.

He was closer now, I could make out a dark figure in the distance, his face only lighting up when the lightning struck the sky.

"I can't help you," he yelled. His voice was somber in a way that made me stop in my tracks. "I can't help you, Jade. You have to get out."

I knew that was the end. I don't know how I knew, but I knew. I quit running. Quit fighting. And instead, I sank to my knees in the thick mud.

This was the end.

CHAPTER 13
Malachi

Jade wasn't next to me when I woke up.

I sat up in a panic, making sure everyone else was still asleep, before I whispered her name in the darkness.

"Jade?" I whispered. "Are you out there?"

I looked to Adonis, who was supposed to wake me up after two hours. He was fast asleep on his log.

I kicked him in the leg, jolting him awake as I walked into the woods. "Where is she?" I asked Adonis. "Jade, where did she go?"

He stammered, giving his answer without having to say a word.

"Jade!" I whispered. No response.

But she was close. I could feel it.

I stepped into the darkness, the low embers of the fire barely helping as my eyes adjusted to the night.

Jade wouldn't be able to see a thing. She was human. This would be nothing but darkness to her.

I closed my eyes and took a deep breath, letting my senses stretch to the forest around me.

Jade was here. She was close. She was alive.

Think, Malachi. Focus.

My power flared around me, and I took another breath to reel it back in. I know I wouldn't hurt Jade, even if I did lose control.

But the others... I wasn't so sure.

I weaved through the trees, careful to be as silent as night as I drifted around the clearing.

I listened for her breath. Her heart beat.

And then I heard her.

"Please," she whimpered. "Please, don't."

I took five steps forward, and I saw her.

Her eyes were open, but they looked vacantly into the nothingness of the night.

"I've given enough," she whispered to nobody.

She had to be asleep. Sleep walking, as they called it.

I stepped forward, careful not to make a sound.

"No," she said, louder this time.

"Jade—" I spoke.

"No!"

"JADE!"

She dropped to her knees in the darkness, a sob of heartbreak leaving her body.

The sound alone froze me to my core.

It was the sound of deep, irrevocable suffering.

And Jade wasn't even awake.

"Wake up," I said, rushing to her side. "Wake up, Jade. You're dreaming."

Another sob wrecked her body. She collapsed entirely, losing all control of herself. I held her shoulders up.

"Wake up!" I yelled again.

She went completely limp then, her head rolling onto my shoulder.

"Jade," I pleaded, no longer hiding the desperation in my voice. "Wake up, please."

She blinked her eyes open and looked at me in the darkness.

Tears streamed down her face. "Malachi?" she breathed. Her voice cracked, which evoked an emotion within me I didn't even know I was capable of feeling.

"I'm right here," I whispered. "I'm right here, Jade."

Small hands wrapped around my waist. Jade's head crashed into my chest as she cried.

And cried.

I wasn't going to let go. I held onto her tightly, like she was the only thing holding me to this world.

"Breathe, Jade," I whispered. "You were sleeping. It was just a dream."

She sobbed again, but took one shaky deep breath.

"Breathe again, Jade."

She did.

"Again."

She took another breath and lifted her head, looking me in my eyes.

Jade opened her mouth to say something, likely to

explain what had happened or what she was so afraid of, but no words came out.

"You don't have to explain anything to me," I whispered. "I know."

I knew my brothers were likely awake now. I knew they had probably found us in the woods and were lingering in the darkness.

I didn't care.

Jade's hand moved to my chest, where my heart was now pounding furiously. "You're here," she whispered to herself. "You're here."

"I'm here, Jade," I repeated. "We're okay."

Minute after minute, her breath became more even.

"Are you ready to go back?" I whispered after some time.

She nodded.

I moved to stand up, but Jade held tightly onto my arm. "Don't leave me," she said. She was awake now, but a soft haze of emotions I couldn't read shadowed her features.

"I'm not going anywhere," I responded. Her legs shook as she stood up, so I bent down and picked her up, carrying her back to camp in my arms.

Jade didn't object. She buried her face in my chest as I walked us back to the fire.

To my surprise, everyone was still fast asleep.

Besides Adonis, who stood at the edge of the camp with a look of concern.

"You're taking my watch now, too, dumb ass," I whispered as I walked by him.

I set Jade down on her own blanket. She settled in immediately, still barely conscious. I relaxed on the ground next to her, close enough to feel if she got up in the night.

We had a few hours left until daylight.

Jade wandering into the forest again while she slept was not an option.

"Go to sleep," I whispered in the darkness. The embers of the fire glowed softly.

Jade didn't respond. Didn't say another word. Simply shut her eyes and went back to sleep.

My heart was racing. Saints. Jade could have easily wandered deep enough into the woods that nobody would have found her. Or worse—where the deadlings found her. Or any other horrific beast dwelling in these parts.

Sleepwalking. That was new.

Nightmares, too.

I would have to keep a close eye on her for the rest of our journey.

A sick feeling sat in the depths of my stomach. I hated that she was afraid.

Did she have nightmares before she ever came to Rewyth? Did she dream about her family? About that bastard of a father beating her?

I stopped myself from clenching my fists as I stared into the dark abyss above.

I was going to make things right. I didn't know how, but I would. I would start by ending things with my father.

My brothers had a plan, but after talking with them earlier in the night, they were desperate for help. They needed someone with power. Someone with control.

They needed me.

The only problem was, as soon as Jade was somewhere safe and away from this mess, I was going to walk straight into Rewyth and kill him myself.

He had to know that. He had to know I was coming for him. Unless of course he still thought I was weak.

He had underestimated me many times before. That wasn't going to be happening again.

But I had other things to handle first. Trithen wasn't exactly going to welcome us with open arms, no matter what those messengers may have said. We would have trouble waiting.

Which meant Jade would still be in danger.

And Sadie and Isaiah...

Isaiah had crossed the line one too many times, like a child playing with a match.

He was going to get himself hurt.

I stayed that way, laying in the darkness, listening to every miniscule noise that the forest made, until my eyelids drifted shut.

And I slept.

CHAPTER 14
Jade

I blinked my eyes open, only to find myself practically draped over Malachi.

Our legs were tangled under the blanket, and I had been using his chest as a pillow.

Saints.

I gently removed the arm that was draped around my body and began to stand. Everyone else was still asleep.

Except for Serefin, who appeared to be on watch.

"Morning," he greeted me as I walked by. "Did you sleep well?"

He must not have woken up during my little episode last night. That's what I was going to call it. An episode. Because there is no way I was going to sleep walk like an idiot into the forest ever again.

"Like a rock," I lied. He eyed me carefully, perhaps he knew I was lying. Serefin was one of the smart ones in the group.

He was also the type of person that would lie about it just to make me feel better.

The others began to stir awake.

Including Esther.

I couldn't even look at her. I couldn't think about her right now.

Not after that nightmare.

I only remembered small portions of it, but I remembered enough to know that she was there. And it wasn't good.

But she had just saved my life in the river. That was twice now that she had saved me. She wasn't going to hurt me.

"I'm going to wash up," I announced before walking toward the river.

I needed a clear mind. I had much of the trip left ahead, and I couldn't afford to crack.

There was too much at risk.

I walked over to the river and knelt down, dipping my hands into the cool morning stream. It was refreshing, and although the night had been cold and the morning was still brisk, I wanted more.

I cupped the water and splashed it into my face.

It was just a dream, I told myself. Esther was still fast asleep. She had slept around the fire like everyone else. They would have seen something.

It was crazy, anyway. To think that Esther had something to do with my nightmare.

Why wouldn't she just warn me of things in

person? Sending a premonition in the form of a nightmare was not only cruel, it was useless.

I shook my head. I was thinking too much. I was thinking about everything too much.

I had no idea how long I had been sleepwalking last night, but I had the faintest memory of Mal finding me.

Thank the Saints it was him, too.

If I had wandered in the wrong direction in the middle of the night...

I didn't let my mind go there. I had been near death many times in my life. Last night was nothing special.

I splashed more water in my face.

"Long night?" Isaiah's voice made me jump. I wiped as much of the water off my skin before replying.

"Not long enough," I answered, keeping things casual. "Just ready to get moving."

"Me too," he responded. "Things are going to be different when we get to Trithen."

He walked forward and knelt next to me. A little too close, but perhaps I was just tense. "What do you mean?"

"You'll see," he answered. "But I think it's important to remember that we're on the same side, you and I. It wouldn't be so terrible if we worked together, would it?"

I shook my head. "You're a mysterious man, Isaiah. I wish you would just say what you mean instead of talking in riddles."

Isaiah dipped his own hands into the steam and

brought them to his mouth, taking a short sip of the water.

"One day, maybe," he mumbled.

I sighed. "One day maybe what?" Frustration pulsed through my body, a hot wave that demanded answers. Esther. Isaiah. Sadie. Malachi. It was too much now. People were going to start answering me, whether they liked it or not.

I slapped the rest of the water out of Isaiah's hands. "Tell me right now," I insisted. "Forget this 'maybe' shit. Start talking."

Isaiah looked at me in surprise, then laughed.

He laughed.

"You're a smart girl, Jade. You know how to get what you want. That's a rare quality, believe it or not. Many people don't have the brains to think for themselves."

"Yet you do?"

"Yes," he replied quickly. "I do. And I think you could be very useful to me."

"Yes, you've implied that."

"And I can help you, too," he said.

"Yes, you implied that, as well. Very vaguely, I might add. More riddles."

"You want me to stop the riddles? Just tell you exactly what I'm thinking right now?"

A heart beat passed. "Yes," I answered.

"Fine," he breathed. "I think you're amazing, Jade. More than amazing. You're the one we've been waiting on for generations. I want you. I need you. I think we could be amazing together, and I curse every damn day that I didn't find you before him. Because I wish every day that you were mine instead."

I had to admit. Of all the things I was expecting him to say, that was not one of them.

My mind went blank.

I opened my mouth to respond, but words failed me. Isaiah waited expectantly, but Saints. What did he think I was going to say? This was absolute shit.

Sadie chose that moment to step into the clearing. "Isaiah," she said. "Esther is looking for you."

The odds of her not having heard everything we just said was low.

Very low.

Isaiah stared at me for a second longer before standing up and walking back to camp.

I stood up and prepared myself for Sadie's wrath. She might have denied any romance business between the two of them, but I was no idiot.

"Sadie, I–"

"Save it," she interrupted. "You don't have to say anything. I know."

"You know what?" She sighed, walking over to the river. "I know he's interested in you, Jade. He would be a fool not to be."

"What do you mean?" I asked.

"He's the leader of Fearford, Jade. You have something that can help him. You're not only favored, you're protected. That's not going to change. You're an asset to him."

I shook my head, hardly able to comprehend what I was hearing.

"Honestly, Sadie," I started, "I don't know how you put up with that. He makes me worried for the entire human race."

She smiled, but it didn't reach her eyes. "He has good intentions, Jade. I know you might not see it, but he does."

"Malachi won't like this."

"He doesn't have to know."

"He's my *husband*," I replied, shocked at how fierce I sounded with the word husband.

Sadie stared at me for a second, almost like she was surprised at my words. Did she think I wouldn't be loyal to Malachi? That I would ditch our marriage as soon as I was in the hands of humans who may want to protect me? Or was it the fact that they saw a weakness and they were willing to take it?

"Whatever," I mumbled to her. "We should go. They're waiting for us."

Sadie responded something as I brushed past her, but I didn't listen long enough to hear the words. Malachi was right. We couldn't trust them. They wanted something from us, and they would stop at nothing to get it.

I tried to neutralilze my face as I walked into the crowd of the Weyland brothers, accompanied now by Esther and Isaiah.

Saints save me.

"Everything okay?" Malachi whispered.

"Fine," I responded. Memories of his arms around me in the middle of the night flashed through my mind. "Everything's fine."

He eyed me, clearly not believing a word I said, but said nothing.

His dark eyes held promise that we would discuss this later.

"Alright," Adonis yelled to the group. "The sun's about up. Let's get moving! We have a ways to go before we arrive at Trithen, and we don't want to be late."

We nodded in agreement and resumed as we were, as if nothing had happened. As if everything was okay. As if everything was the same as it was yesterday.

But it wasn't the same. And everything was far from being okay.

CHAPTER 15
Malachi

"No. We were invited here. We'll walk in like the guests we are."

The others looked at me like I had just asked them to walk onto a battlefield. The only one who didn't was Jade.

Jade. Who may have been equally as suicidal as myself.

My heart was pounding in my ears. I ignored it. I also ignored the loud voice in my mind that told me this was a mistake.

That voice was lying.

I was Malachi Weyland, heir to the fae throne and the deadly Prince of Shadows. If these bastards demanded to speak with me, I would allow them the privilege.

But my friends and family had nothing to fear.

I took a deep breath and tapped into the rumbling power I now felt in my chest. It waited patiently for my command, just like it had done every day now for decades.

It had never once let me down. It wasn't going to start today.

"Can I talk to you for a second?" Jade asked me.

"Right now?" I asked.

"Yes. Right now."

The urgency in her voice forced me to listen. I nodded, and followed her into the safety of the treeline.

"What's wrong?" I asked as soon as we were out of ear shot. "Are you okay?"

"I'm fine," she answered quickly. "I'm okay, it's okay. I just..."

"What?"

"I just have a weird feeling about this, Mal. And I know we came all this way and the last thing you want is someone else questioning your decision to come here, but I just wanted to look you in the eyes and tell you myself. So that maybe you could look me in the eyes back and tell me that I was being crazy, that I had nothing to fear."

I smiled. I couldn't help it. "Well, you're right about one thing, princess. You are crazy."

She tried to smile back but stepped forward. She was close enough now I could still smell the slight scent of cinnamon lingering in her hair, even after our long journey.

It was intoxicating.

"If anything happens in there—"

"Stop," I interrupted. "Don't talk like that."

"And don't interrupt me."

I shut up.

"If anything happens in there, Malachi, I want you to know that this little arrangement has been more than a surprise to me. You've been pleasantly different than I imagined. And you've saved my life countless times, which you never had to do. And I don't know if I properly thanked you or not, but this might be my last chance. So, thank you."

It took me a second to find my words. "Wow," I responded. "Jade Farrow thanking me? Am I dead already?"

"It's not funny!" she said, but a real smile crept into her features. "Whatever they want, Malachi, just give it to them. I don't care what it is. We pretend like we're on their side, and as soon as we leave this place, we'll make a plan to deal with it. To deal with everything."

A wave of relief hit me. Relief that Jade didn't think I was a complete monster. That she cared about what was going to happen next. And that somewhere inside of her, she wanted to help me survive this thing, too.

"We can't trust the others," I said. "Whatever they want from us here, it won't be good. Isaiah, my mother. They have their own agendas. I can feel it. I just don't know what they are yet."

"The truth will come out."

"The truth will come out," I repeated.

Jade moved to walk away, saying, "We should probably get back."

I caged her against the tree with my arms, pressing my body lightly into hers. "Not yet," I whispered.

A flicker of satisfaction crossed her eyes.

It was the same look I had seen on her the first time I saw her in the forest of her home. Jade held a darkness inside of her that wanted her to survive, no matter how badly she wanted to believe otherwise at times. It was what made us so alike. I saw the darkest parts of myself in her.

I just hoped she wouldn't run away when she saw the same in me.

"Kiss me already," she whispered, her deep brown eyes blinking up at me.

I obeyed.

Her lips were gentle and soft against mine. The kiss wasn't a declaration of love or a desperate need for physical touch. It was simply a kiss. A promise that Jade was mine, and I was hers.

And for now, that would be enough.

"Let's go, lovebirds," Adeline's voice yelled from the trees. "We don't have all day!"

Jade smiled as I pulled away, silently cursing that we didn't have more time for this.

More time to just be Jade and Malachi. Husband and wife.

"We'll resume this later," Jade promised.

"I'm counting on it."

And then it was over. Back to business. Back to masks and charades and running around like pawns in a game.

And the game was only beginning.

We walked forward in unison. Jade and I led the pack with my brothers and Adeline behind us, followed by Esther, Sadie and Isaiah.

We walked for a few minutes before a familiar figure stepped into view.

"You came!" the leader of Trithen sang as we approached the towering gates. His face brought back hundreds of memories of my time here.

Seth. The King of Trithen.

I only knew he was their leader because I had met him before.

And it hadn't been a friendly introduction.

Memories of war flashed through my mind, of hundreds, if not thousands, of fae dying on the battlefield over nothing but power.

Power that this man's family once wanted.

Power that the fae of Rewyth possessed.

"We did," I replied. My wings flared around my body, Jade standing partially behind my right wing. His eyes settled on them, as if he was just remembering exactly who he was dealing with.

The owner of the black wings. The wielder of the dark powers.

The Prince of Shadows.

"Although," I continued, "I must admit we were rather comfortable in Fearford with our new friends here. May I ask what business required us to travel all this way?"

"Not now," he replied. "Let's get your new friends here settled in, and then we'll discuss business."

I clenched my fists at my side. I could have sent him to his knees. I could have released a power so forceful that his heart eventually stopped from the pain.

But then where would we be?

"That's very generous of you," Esther spoke up from behind me. "We thank you for your hospitality. We'll talk about business later."

She sounded kind and light, but her last words were a threat.

"Please," he said, motioning to the group. "I've had the divine pleasure of meeting the Weyland gentleman, but I'm afraid the rest of you are strangers to me."

Isaiah stepped forward immediately, like a pet pouncing for a piece of meat. "I'm Isaiah. My father was Vincent, leader of Fearford."

The man looked Isaiah up and down before extending his hand.

It was a sure sign of respect. Fae didn't shake hands with humans lightly.

And for good reason.

"And this is my partner, Sadie. She helps me run things in Fearford."

Sadie shook his hand but said nothing.

When the others didn't speak up, I spoke up for them. "This is my mother, Esther. My sister, Adeline. And my wife, Jade."

They all nodded respectively but said nothing.

That didn't stop Seth's eyes from lingering on Jade, likely drinking in her human features.

"What I've been told holds true?" he started. "The others will be very intrigued by this... union."

"It's nothing that breaks any treaties," I defended.

"No?" he asked. "And how does the lovely bride feel about that?"

Jade stiffened behind me. I resisted the urge to grab her hand, but the last thing I needed to do was exhibit my weakness in new territory.

"She feels just fine about it, thank you for asking," I retorted before Jade spoke up. My brothers snickered behind me.

"Very well, then," Seth continued. He turned and led us through the gate. "There will be a Spring Festival this evening. I encourage you each to join us. After your long trip, it's the least we can do."

I nodded politely, the others did the same. Seth continued talking about the history of Trithen, explaining pointless facts that the others pretended to care about.

As soon as our business was over, I would unleash my power.

For Jade's sake, I had to hold it together.

Seth brought us inside the massive walls of Trithen. They were similar to Rewyth's, just like I remembered them to be. Of course, no height of walls could keep out a fae who was determined to enter.

But the walls were to keep out other things.

The fae had *some* enemies, after all.

"You can take the bed," I said to Jade after we were escorted to our rooms.

She laughed, but not a real Jade laugh. It was more of a nervous laugh, one I rarely heard from her.

"What's wrong?" I asked.

"You're my husband," she replied. "You don't have to sleep on the floor. I think we can both be adults here."

"Really?" I teased.

"Yes. Unless you disagree, then by all means sleep on the hard floor."

"Please," I teased. "I am much older than you, you know. If one of us is capable of acting like an adult, it's surely me."

She smiled half-heartedly, but her face grew dark just moments later.

"Something's wrong," I insisted. "Tell me what it is."

Jade turned her eyes to the ceiling, blinking away tears. "It's nothing," she said.

"It's clearly something," I pushed. "If something is bothering you, just tell me and I'll handle it."

She shook her head, a single tear dropping down her tan skin. "No, it's not like that. It's just..." She paused and looked at me with those deep, ocean eyes. "Today is my birthday. I'm officially eighteen."

My breath escaped me.

"And I'm sure Tessa is somewhere spending my birthday alone, thinking about all the possible ways I could have been killed by now. Or better yet, happily married to a monster."

Her words didn't hurt me. They were true. I saw the way Jade's sister had looked at her...like there was a stranger in Jade's own skin.

Tessa was the one person Jade had fought to survive for when she first came to Rewyth.

I didn't let another second go by. I crossed the room in two steps and wrapped my arms around her. She did the same in return, as if she were desperate for it. "Happy birthday, princess," I whispered. I was glad she couldn't see my face, the disgust that would be dripped all over it.

Not disgust at her, of course.

I felt disgusted with myself, that I had let my own wife's birthday pass and she could do nothing but sit by and watch.

"I'll make it up to you," I said to her. "I promise I will."

"I don't care about my birthday anyway," she responded. "It's never been more than disappointment and the depressing thought that I am yet another year closer to my death."

I couldn't respond.

"Things might be changing now that I married you and am still alive."

Still, I said nothing.

"You can talk, you know," she responded. "It's not like I blame you for any of this."

"No," I said eventually, "but that doesn't mean any of it is okay. You can be angry. Saints, you *should* be angry. With me or with the fae. You're allowed to be mad."

Jade shook her head. "If anything, I feel guilty."

"Guilty?"

She nodded. "It's almost as if, when I was home with my father and Tessa, I was waiting to die. But now, with you and the others, with people who actually care if I come home at night or if I'm stranded in the middle of the woods...I've never felt more *alive*."

I knew exactly how she felt. Like her family wasn't really her family. Like she was never really accepted before. But now...

"I get it," I whispered. "I do."

"I know you do."

We stayed like that for a while, I held her in my arms tightly to my chest until tears no longer threatened her eyes. "Okay," She started. "It's been a long day, and I'm sure we have a very long night ahead of us."

"That's an understatement," I responded. "There's probably a few things we should go over before we throw you into a fae party."

"Will it be like our wedding?" she asked.

"It will and it won't."

I wanted to tell her about the previous war with Trithen, about how these fae were vicious in ways that made the fae in Rewyth look like saints.

But Jade had no more reason to worry.

"Why don't you try to rest a bit before the festival?"

"And where are you going?"

"I have an errand to run. I won't be long. But don't go to that festival without me, Jade. I'll come back for you."

She stared at me like she knew I was lying. "Don't do anything stupid, Malachi. We don't want to start trouble."

I let my dark wings flare, just slightly, so she remembered they were there. "Don't forget, princess. You've married the Prince of Shadows. I was born starting trouble."

Jade rolled her eyes, but walked to the bathroom and shut the door behind her.

We had a few hours before the party officially started, which meant I had plenty of time to track down Seth and get the business over with before any fae tricks were involved.

And I had to do it before anyone got any ideas about messing with Jade.

I left our room, making sure the door was completely shut before walking across the hall and knocking. "Adeline, it's me," I announced.

"What do you want?" she responded. "Saints, I just laid down!"

"I need you to stay with Jade for a bit. Can you do that?"

She cursed under her breath, but I heard footsteps approaching the door.

She swung it open, clearly not satisfied about being interrupted. "Fine," she said. "Where are you going?"

"I have some business to take care of."

Adeline laughed, but grabbed my arm before I could turn and walk away. "Oh no you don't," she said. "We all got dragged here because of you, so you don't get to go off alone on some secret mission and not tell me what's going on," she said. "Spill it."

I shook my head. Adeline had always been this stubborn, so I wasn't sure why it surprised me now.

"Fine," I said. "I have old business with Seth. I just want to talk to him and make sure it won't cause any problems with whatever he wants from us now."

Adeline released my arm, only to smack me in the chest. "What was that for!"

"That was for you being an idiot, Mal! Are you kidding me?"

"What do you mean?"

She stepped forward and lowered her voice. "You'll start another war, and we both know it."

"Don't be ridiculous," I replied, knowing that her words did hold some truth. Any of us stepping out of line could start a war. Our political history with Trithen had been that patchy.

"I'm not being ridiculous, Mal. I'm being logical.

You killed his father, for Saint's sake. That's not something that a man just forgets."

I rubbed a hand down my face, trying to hide my annoyance. "I'm aware, Adeline. Very aware."

"Fine," she responded after a few seconds. "But if you go and get us all killed, that's on you."

I rolled my eyes and backed away, beginning to walk back down the hallway. "Watch her closely, Adeline," I yelled without turning around. She mumbled something in response. I didn't wait to see if she would go to Jade's room, I knew she would. Not only was Adeline the only sibling capable of taking orders from me, but she genuinely cared about Jade's safety. And not because of some stupid blood oath, either. She actually cared about Jade.

I shoved her words out of my mind. I had no time for that. No time for fear. No time for reminiscing on the past.

"And where are you heading?" Serefin's voice echoed down the hall just as I was about to exit the building. "Storming into the heart of Trithen for a stroll, then?"

I cursed under my breath, but I was certain he heard it. "Not you, too, Ser. Not now."

Ser shook his head and marched toward me down the hall.

"No," he said. "I'm not letting my prince walk around Trithen alone. Whatever you have to do, I'm coming with you."

Saints. I suppose I should have expected Serefin of

all people to be on my side, to not convince me to back down. "You don't have to do this," I replied.

Ser clasped a hand on my shoulder and squeezed. "Neither do you," was all he said.

"Saints, Ser. it's not like I'm going to storm out there and kill them all."

"I wouldn't put it above you, brother. Let's just go get it over with, okay? I'm with you."

I'm with you.

Words I had heard from Serefin a half a dozen times. Ser had followed me into war. More than once. He had killed for me. He had saved my life. He had put himself before me hundreds of times.

This was just another one of those times.

"Fine," I said. "Let's go."

We turned, and the two of us walked out of the castle and into the blazing sunset.

"Seth can't be trusted. Whatever business he wants to deal with, we can deal with it now," I whispered to Ser. We had to be careful, though. Too many fae ears surrounded us.

Trithen, like any fae city, shined with beauty. Similar to Rewyth, nature ran through every piece of architecture. Where Rewyth was dark and green, though, Trithen reminded me of spring. Red, pink and orange flowers twisted around endless vines, matching the glow of the sunset that reflected off the white, stone buildings.

It hadn't looked this clean during war. The white walls had been splattered with blood.

Most of it I had spilled. Some of it had been my army.

All of it had been deserved.

Images of Seth's father falling to his knees before me flashed through my brain. I had killed him, too. Simply another number to add to my total. Simply politics.

Trithen had a lesson to learn at the time.

I had hoped Seth remembered the consequences of his father.

Serefin must have remembered, too. Remembered this place shining red, but not from the sunset. He tensed as we walked past the center of the city, the same place we had forced everyone to bow before us, and the same place we had killed everyone who resisted.

Like I said. Politics.

Messy, messy politics.

"You know where you're going?" Ser whispered to me. We turned one last corner and approached a large building with a solid, stone door. Two guards stood on each side, all four of them immediately drawing their swords when we approached.

As if that could stop us.

"I'm pretty sure, yeah," I whispered back to Ser.

We approached the guards with caution.

"What do you want?" one of them asked. I saw the way their eyes all flickered to my black wings. And the way the grips on their weapons tightened.

I smiled.

"I would like to speak with Seth. He should be expecting me," I lied.

The guards didn't flinch. "Nobody is being expected," they said.

That was confirmation that Seth was in here.

"You're wrong," I said, clasping my hands behind my back and lifting my chin. "Seth has asked me to come here, and I'm a bit late. So, if you could just–"

"Turn around," he interrupted. "Nobody's getting past this door. Especially Rewyth scum."

I took a breath.

I counted to three.

The power that rumbled through my body begged for a release, it knew I wanted it, too.

So, this time, I let it go. I pictured each of the guards dropping to their knees in pain, screaming for mercy.

They did.

I pictured them scratching their own faces, wanting to dig into their own eyeballs to stop the pain in their brains.

They did.

I kept it going, too. Serefin whispered something behind me but I didn't stop. Had they forgotten who I was? The Prince of Shadows. Had they forgotten what I could do?

More pain. More misery. More power.

The stone door slammed open behind the guards.

"That's enough," Seth's voice boomed the area, echoing off the walls of buildings around us.

I let my power linger, a fraction longer of a second, before pulling it back in with a simple breath.

The guards moaned in pain, but would be fine. My power never caused real physical damage, it only made them think they were dying, burning from the inside out.

I assumed it was misery.

"Hello," I said to Seth. "I was just telling your guards here that I would like to speak with you."

"And this is how you treat your hosts?" he responded. Anger laced his words, but I saw his heart racing.

Fear.

Good. He should be afraid of me. Every bastard in this damned city should fear me.

I walked past the guards and approached Seth.

"You want to talk business?" I said quietly, inches from his face. "Let's talk, shall we?"

Seth was pissed. More than pissed. I had walked openly through his kingdom, dropped four of his guards to their knees with nothing more than a thought, and demanded to speak to him.

But he didn't have much of a choice.

"Fine," He agreed. He glanced at Serefin behind me, then turned for us to follow. "This way."

I glanced back at Ser, who only shook his head in disapproval. Except a small smile on his face told me something else.

"Perfect," I said, clapping my hands together as we

followed. My large wings tucked tightly behind me as we maneuvered the hallway.

We arrived at what I assumed was Seth's library, Ser and I both taking a seat along a large wooden table.

Seth didn't sit. He only paced the room before us.

"So," I started when he never did. "You invited us here for a reason. To see if my marriage with Jade was legitimate. To see if we were breaking the treaties. Well we aren't, you've seen that. Yet we're still here."

Seth nodded. "And what would your father say about all of this? About living with the humans?"

"Don't speak to me about my father," I replied.

"The King of Rewyth, you mean?" Seth retorted.

Seth laughed quietly. "That is supposed to be your position soon, is it not? I can't help but wonder why you're parading around Fearford, a human kingdom. Shouldn't you be home, preparing to take the throne?"

"I prepare for the throne every day, Seth. Every single second is yet another second closer to becoming King."

"And where does that leave your human wife, Prince? Beside you on the throne?"

I merely nodded.

Seth shook his head again. "Your father will never allow it."

"How would you know what my father will and will not allow?"

"I am no idiot, despite what you may think. The King of Rewyth is many things, but a supporter of humans is not one of them. That's why he sent you to live with them in Fearford, isn't it? To destroy them all? To overpower them? Or maybe just to slaughter them all like you've done before."

Serefin stiffened beside me.

"I figured as much," Seth continued. "Humans and fae together, it will never last. You know this."

"And you brought us all the way here for what, exactly? A friendly warning?"

Seth eyed me, and moved to take a seat at the table across from us. "No," he said. "That's not all."

Serefin and I waited for more.

"We know about Jade."

My power rumbled. I didn't move a muscle.

"We know she's... special. That some believe she is to fulfill some sort of prophecy for the witches."

"The witches believe in many different prophecies, Seth," I stated, sounding as bored as I possibly could. "I can only imagine what else they think about Jade."

Seth shook his head. "If what they're saying is true..."

"What?" I pushed. "You'll keep her for yourself? Is that it?"

"No," He said. "No. If what they say is true, and Jade is the peacemaker, then we could work together."

Serefin snorted a laugh beside me. I hardly did the same.

"Work together?" I repeated. "And do what, exactly?"

Seth eyed me for a moment before saying, "You're a killer, Malachi. I, of all people, know that."

A silent pause filled the air.

"But I also know that you are much smarter than the King of Rewyth. And I know who gives the orders."

Still, I didn't respond.

"You better be very careful about what you're saying," Serefin warned.

Seth put his hands out on the table in front of us. "I didn't call you here for more fighting," he said. "I brought you here because I wanted to know if the whispers were true. If they are true, if Jade is the peacemaker and she is here to fulfill the prophecy, you'll want help protecting her. Every single kingdom on this planet will come for her, and you know it."

"Including Trithen."

"Not if we have what we want."

"Which is what, exactly?"

"Peace."

That was unexpected.

"You're a wealthy fae kingdom. You have peace," I replied slowly.

He nodded again. "Our enemies threaten us every single day. We're fighting for resources, mostly because Rewyth has cut most of our supply chains. These people may live in ignorance, Prince Malachi, but I won't be able to hide it for long. If we help to protect Jade from whatever is coming, if we work together, then when you become King of Rewyth, you will open all trading docks to Trithen again, how it once was."

I hated the thought, but Seth actually made some sense. Perhaps Trithen truly *did* need our help.

"This is all based on some story my mother is telling. How can you be sure that what they say in the prophecy is true?"

"We have very powerful witches working with us, Prince. We are not wrong, and neither is your mother."

I took a deep breath. I needed to talk to my mother. If the other kingdoms would came after Jade, having Trithen on our side wouldn't be the worst idea.

"We know you can't go back to Rewyth," Seth said. A hint of sympathy lined his words.

"That's not true," I replied. "I can go back any time."

"And Jade? My sources tell me your father was not her biggest fan the last time they interacted. How's Jade's back doing, by the way?"

I stood so fast my chair fell backwards behind me. "Do not speak of that," I growled. "Ever."

Serefin was at my side in an instant, grabbing my arm and holding me back.

As if that would stop my power if I dared to use it.

As if *anyone* could stop me.

"I apologize," Seth said. "I meant no offense. Just trying to verify some rumors, that's all."

Rumors. That was the last thing I wanted to deal with.

"If you kill your own father, Malachi, you will start a war. And you have no army. You have no backing. Work with us, and we will fight by your side. We will help you kill him. You will become the next King of Rewyth, you will sit on the most powerful fae throne. And Trithen and Rewyth can be at peace again. That is what I'm proposing. That is why I invited you here."

The tension in the air was palpable.

"Think about it," Seth said. "Talk to your mother. We have all evening to relax and enjoy yourselves. We'll discuss this again later."

Serefin and I turned to leave, but I couldn't quite make myself take my next step. I turned back around and looked at Seth.

"Why?" I asked. "Why would you help us? I killed your father."

Seth didn't blink. "I remember what you did," he said. "But I had a father and a king giving me orders once, too. Let's just say that I'm hoping things can be different."

CHAPTER 16

Jade

I looked ridiculous, but I expected nothing less.

My dress covered more skin than my wedding gown in Rewyth had, but it wasn't much of a difference.

Adeline gasped as I exited the bathroom, covering her mouth with her hand.

"Stunning," she responded. She then proceeded to squeal in excitement and clap her hands. "Just gorgeous, Jade! You'll be turning the heads of every male in this kingdom."

"Oh, fun," I mumbled. "I can't wait."

She turned me around to face a large mirror that leaned against the wall. "Look at you!" she whispered in awe. I took a look at my gown, covered in red and orange flowers, white lace, and not much else. I looked like spring threw up on me.

"This looks absurd," I responded. "Are you sure this is what we're supposed to wear tonight?"

Adeline had a similar dress on, covered in pink flowers that screamed spring. *That was Trithen*, she had explained to me.

And tonight's festival was to celebrate just that–spring.

"It's the Spring Festival," she replied. "I promise you, Jade, we'll be the least ridiculous looking people here. Besides, everyone will be too wasted to notice."

Great.

"Are you sure it's a good idea for me to go? The fae here can't be fans of humans either, I assume."

"Trust me, you'll be protected. I won't let you out of my sight. Malachi would kill me if I did."

My long hair fell down to my waist in loose curls, similar to Adeline's. Her face glowed with a hint of the sun from our journey.

My stomach erupted in butterflies.

Saints. Was I really nervous?

"You'll be fine," Adeline said, as if she could read my thoughts. "We'll show up, eat, drink, dance, and it'll be over before you know it. You might even be sad that it's over. Kingdoms all over the planet speak of Trithen Festivals, you know."

"Really?" I asked. "Why?"

Adeline grabbed both of my hands and pulled me toward the bedroom door. The sun had just set, and the call of sweet music flowed through the open window. "I guess we'll be finding out soon," she answered. "Let's go!"

I pulled back. "Malachi didn't want me to leave without him. I should wait."

Adeline rolled her eyes. "You're with me," she said. "You'll be fine, Jade. And if he gets all pissed off and protective, you can blame me. He's probably already down there, anyway!"

I hated that Adeline could convince me so easily, but she was right. I wasn't going to wait up in this room like some sort of helpless girl waiting for her savior.

I was going to the festival.

Adeline knew what I had decided as soon as I smiled.

And soon enough, we were headed out the door.

"This is amazing!" Adeline yelled in my ear. I could hardly hear her over the loud violins booming through the air around us. Saints, I didn't even know those instruments could play so loudly.

Adrenaline pulsed through my body. All around us, fae were covered in spring-colored jewels, dresses, and anything else they seemed to find. Silver and white wings covered the entire field, and fires around the perimeter allowed my human eyes to see in the darkness.

She was right. It was stunning.

Singing, dancing, laughing, eating. Hundreds of

men and women littered the field. Nobody seemed to care that I was human, or that Adeline was from Rewyth. Nobody even glanced in our direction.

Perhaps this wouldn't be as bad as I thought it would be.

"Come on, Jade," Adeline said, pulling me toward a massive table of food and drinks.

She picked up a goblet of wine for herself, then handed one over to me.

"Is this okay for humans to drink?" I asked her, remembering the warnings I had been given about fae wine in Rewyth.

Adeline shook her head. "It's a festival, Jade. I won't tell if you don't."

I smiled. I loved this side of Adeline. She was nothing like her brothers. Her brothers were sneaky and stubborn. Adeline was wild, free, and alive.

I aspired to be like that. To be free.

To be alive.

I took the drink from her, and she cheered once more. Adeline's energy was contagious, there was no way I could say no to her.

We both took a small sip, and Adeline watched me carefully as I swallowed.

It didn't burn like I had expected it to. In fact, the drink was especially sweet. "Wow," I said, taking another sip. "This tastes surprisingly good!"

Adeline nodded and took another drink herself. "And the more you drink, the better it gets," she whispered.

We both laughed.

"Happy birthday, by the way," she whispered in my ear. "Malachi has a loud mouth."

I started to argue with her, but shut my mouth. It *was* my birthday. There was a time when I thought I would never live long enough to see this day. I deserved to enjoy myself tonight. "Thank you, Adeline," was all I said.

The cool breeze of night blew past us, blowing my hair off my shoulders.

I felt happy. I didn't want to admit that, and in many ways, it still felt so wrong, but it was true. I felt happy.

"Have you been to a party like this before?" I asked her.

Adeline nodded and hooked her arm through mine as we began walking the perimeter of the field. "I've been to many parties in my lifetime. I spent a decade or two lost in them. It can be exhilarating, yes, but at the end of the day, it's an escape. People like to party this way because they can forget about all their problems for a day. They can forget about war or famine or politics and they can just... be."

I nodded as she talked. Her words made a lot of sense. They were fae, and perhaps things were hundreds of times better in fae kingdoms then they were in human ones, but they still had their issues.

However dumb the humans thought those issues were, comparatively.

"And what were you escaping from?" I asked her.

Adeline smiled as she stared into the distance, but the smile didn't reach her eyes. "Many things," she replied quietly. "It's a miracle I ever came out of it, to be honest," she said.

"Issues with your father?" I pushed.

"Among many things. My father has been very controlling of all of us, not just Malachi. He lets the other boys off easier, yes, but he still wanted control every step of the way. And he wanted to prove his control."

"On you?" I asked. "It always seemed like he ignored you most of the time. He doesn't even include you in politics."

Adeline took a breath and finished the rest of her drink in one sip.

"The only daughter in the Weyland family sounds like a blessing, I know. But hear this, Jade. You and I are similar. We are women. These men will use us in their biddings for anything they please. That doesn't change for me just because I am fae. Nor does it change because I am part of the royal family."

Her voice cracked, and my heart nearly shattered. If I hadn't hated the King with every single ounce of my being before, I certainly did now.

I wanted to ask her what specifically he had made her do. Had he sold her as part of some deal like he had done to me? Traded her? Used her for seduction? Pawned her off like a fancy jewel?

Adeline was powerful and spontaneous. It shocked me that someone so vibrant could have suffered so much, but I saw it now in her eyes. A certain darkness lingered there.

"I'm sorry, Adeline. It's not right what they do."

Adeline rolled her shoulders back and lifted her chin. "No, it's not. But we're here. We're alive. And there's an entire evening ahead of us. We can escape for the night, Jade. We can be free for tonight. So drink that damn glass!"

I obeyed, swallowing the entire glass of liquid in three large sips.

She stared at me with wide eyes when I looked back up. "What?" I asked.

"Malachi's going to kill me," she mumbled, but she laughed.

I looked over my shoulders, making sure he wasn't approaching out of nowhere before answering, "Don't scare me like that!" I laughed.

Adeline shoved my shoulder lightly. "You love him," she said.

I scoffed. "No, I don't."

She rolled her eyes and brought us back to the table of drinks, grabbing another glass for herself. When I reached for one, she cut me off. "Maybe no more for the human, at least for the next hour or so."

"Why?" I asked. "I don't feel a thing."

"Oh, you will," she laughed. "I just hope Malachi shows up before you're passed out in the field."

"Adeline!" I yelled. "I'm going to pass out?"

She tossed her head back and laughed, her curls falling along her back.

Without answering me, she pulled me into the crowd.

This festival, even with the loud music and the group of dancing people, was nothing like the simple bonfire in Fearford. The fae never stopped. Never tired. And the way they danced...

I stared at a group of fae, two girls and a boy, dancing together on the dance floor. The way their bodies moved together, as if all three of them were *involved*.

I blushed and quickly looked away.

"Don't be embarrassed," Adeline said. "Humans are all prudes compared to the fae, remember? It's totally normal here."

I nodded and continued to follow her.

"Come on," she said once we got to the middle of the field. "We're dancing."

She grabbed both of my arms and began dancing slowly, moving to the rhythm of the music just like we had done in Fearford.

Our dresses blended with the massive, colorful crowd under the moon and stars. The sky was shockingly clear, allowing the twinkling of the sky to add to the essence of the festival.

Saints. Perhaps that drink was starting to kick in.

There was hardly space to move in the crowd. Bodies bumped against my back and shoulders, but Adeline didn't let go of me. She wrapped her arms across my shoulders, pulling me close to her as the two of us danced.

A slow warmth moved across my body, starting in my bare feet and working up my legs. It was more than just feeling intoxicated, it was life itself re-entering my body.

I had missed that feeling.

I tossed my head back and laughed. I couldn't help it. Pure euphoria spread slowly across every inch of me.

When I brought my head back up and looked at Adeline, I knew she felt the same way. Her eyes twinkled, reflecting the blanket of stars above us.

"Relax, Jade," she whispered into my ear. "Escape."

I knew exactly what she meant. I closed my eyes, same as her, and let the feeling of magic overtake my body, my motions. With Adeline's body touching mine, I swayed to the music. The violin called to me, like it was playing secretly for my soul and my soul only. Like it was mine alone to enjoy. I laughed and cheered, and nobody stopped to stare. Nobody cared, everyone was too busy living their own euphoria.

Escaping.

Adeline grabbed my hand and spun me in a circle where we stood.

We both laughed when I nearly fell over, large wings behind me bumping me and causing me to fall into her body.

We continued to dance like that, bumping everyone around us and laughing like idiots, until I truly thought my stomach would burst from laughter.

I wanted to tell her to stop, that I needed a break, but I couldn't find the words. It was addicting.

My legs were exhausted, yet they had never felt better. I grabbed Adeline's arm and was about to pull her toward me when strong hands grabbed me roughly from behind.

"Having fun?" Malachi whispered in my ear. He sounded... *not* euphoric.

An interruption in my ecstasy.

I spun around, but his hands didn't leave my body. "Yes," I said, not able to hide the laughter from my voice.

Malachi gave a death glare to Adeline, who only laughed even more. Which caused me to laugh again.

"I told you not to leave without me," he said.

"We're just dancing," Adeline defended. Malachi shot her another glare, as if to send a message.

"Fine," Adeline said. "I'll be dancing over there, come find me when your husband is done being a buzzkill, Jade," she said to me.

And then she was lost in the crowd, leaving Malachi and I clinging to each other in the night.

"How much did you drink?" he asked me.

I shook my head. "Only one cup. I am being very responsible, I swear."

"Adeline knows better. Even a sip is enough for you to trip all night."

I laughed again, then stood on my tippy toes in the grass to wrap my arms around Mal's neck. My feet nearly came off the ground.

"Who cares," I said. "Escape with me."

His hands wrapped around my body, holding me to

him. A low growl rumbled in his chest, but he didn't object.

"Don't tell me you don't want to," I purred. "I know you do. Escape with me, Mal. Dance with me."

It was ludicrous. This was so different from Fearford, when we had been civil and I had been drinking *human* drinks.

This was a dream. Nothing felt real, and yet everything felt right.

With Malachi holding me to him, I tipped my head back and swayed. Laughter bubbled in my chest as the night air blew through my hair. When I lifted my head again, Malachi was staring at me with his lips parted.

"What?" I asked.

He shook his head. "You are breathtaking, Jade Farrow."

"Tell me what you're feeling," he whispered, lips brushing against my ear. A chill ran down my bare spine. "Tell me in detail, and don't leave a single thing out."

Where did I begin? "I feel...I feel alive," I stared, stating the obvious. "I feel weightless. My feet should be hurting but they're tingling with life, like the earth is feeding my soul and my body just wants more."

Malachi leaned in and brushed his lips against my neck, the kiss of a mere feather.

"I feel warm. Not hot, though, just warm. Like my blood is magic, pumping through each of my veins with every passing heartbeat."

"Mhmm," he hummed against my body.

"And I feel free," I said. I leaned back again, holding onto him while I stared up at the stars. They all blurred together now, but I knew they were there. I knew they were shining above us. "Like I could join them," I said.

"The stars?" Malachi asked.

"Yes," I said. "The stars. I want to be as free as the stars."

"Then I will rip this world apart until I can place you in the sky myself, princess."

Emotion overwhelmed me. Logically, I knew it was the fae drink. But I didn't care. Tears bubbled in my eyes before I could even blink them away.

"What?" Malachi asked me. "What's wrong?" I pressed my forehead against his. "Tell me what you're feeling."

"I..."

Saints. I felt confused. I wanted Malachi, I wanted him more than anything. And that scared me. Because I knew I could never have him, not really. Malachi was the fae Prince, and I was nothing but a mere human.

Even if he wanted to set me free, that would mean losing him.

And what world would that be? What type of life would I be living?

"I'll never be free," I admitted to him.

"Don't say that," he said. "You know it's not true."

I shook my head. "You don't understand."

I grabbed his body, pulling him closer and closer to me. As if that would save me. As if we could merge together and become one. "I want this," I whispered to him. "I want you."

Malachi's chest heaved. "Then you have me."

And then his lips crashed into mine.

Malachi was practically carrying me as we were swallowed deeply into the crowd. I wrapped a leg around his waist and he grabbed it, holding me to him.

His mouth was hot and heavy against mine. I was hungry, desperate for more of him. Each place he touched me left a scorching trail of passion, a fire that didn't burn out.

I clung to him, wrapping my arms around his neck and lifting myself up so I could guide him, kissing him with all the emotions I felt in my body. I wanted him. It was true.

And he was here. Kissing me.

Our mouths moving together was just another part of the dance, another part of the dream. Magic.

Malachi's black wings flared out for just an instant, eventually finding a way to surround our bodies. But it wasn't the privacy I wanted.

"Malachi," I whispered, trying to catch my breath between our kisses.

"Yes, princess?" he mumbled against my mouth.

"I want you to take me back to our room," I whispered. I scanned his face, searching for an inch of hesitation.

But all I got was a low purr of approval.

He kissed me again, deeply, before pulling away.

"I want nothing more than to take you upstairs and

do what I've wanted to do since the moment I laid eyes on you, princess," he said.

My stomach swarmed in butterflies. Only for a moment, though, until Malachi's face hardened.

"What?" I asked, pulling away another inch. "What is it?"

"We can't, Jade. I mean...I can't."

I couldn't be hearing this correctly. "What do you mean, you can't?"

He mumbled under his breath before answering. "I don't want to complicate things," he said.

I would have backed up if it weren't for his strong hands holding me tight. "Complicate what, exactly?"

"We should have talked about this before, Jade. What this mess is between us. We've been acting like everything is fine. We've been acting like we can just go on living happily ever after after the politics are handled. But at the end of the day, you're a human. You're a human and I'm a fae."

"Where is this coming from?" I asked. "Why are you suddenly bringing this up?"

"Because we can't ignore it anymore, Jade. We don't have a future, and you need to understand that."

My ears were ringing, louder than the hundreds of thoughts running through my head. This was coming out of nowhere, a complete turn in directions.

Malachi wanted a future with me.

Didn't he?

"Let's just calm down and we can talk about this tomorrow," I said.

PRINCE OF SINS AND SHADOWS

"What will change tomorrow?" he growled. "You'll still be a human, and I'll still be the big, bad fae that forced you into marriage."

"Stop!" I yelled. "You know I don't think of you that way."

"You should. This will never change, Jade. I'm the Prince of Shadows, remember? You'll be safer without me. You'll be safer with someone like Isaiah."

I couldn't believe I just heard him say that. I fought the strong urge I felt to slap him across the face.

"You don't mean that," I said, staggering backward. This time, he let me back away.

"I do," he said. His walls were back up. His eyes were darker than I had ever seen them. "I do mean that, Jade. And you need to listen to me."

Tears threatened my eyes, but I wasn't going to let him see me cry over him.

Not because of this.

I was the one that should be ending this stupid fling we had going on, not him. I was the one that had been ripped from my home and forced to live in Rewyth. I was the one who had suffered because of this union.

Not him. Not Malachi.

I ripped myself away and tore through the crowd. Malachi didn't follow me.

Adrenaline still pulsed through my veins. The way it mixed with the fae drinks had my entire body tingling in a way I couldn't put into words.

Bodies pushed and shoved me from every angle, but nobody stopped me as I continued to make my way through the crowd, back in the direction Adeline and I had come from.

I had to get out of here. I had to clear my mind. I just needed space to think.

Finally, the pool of bodies began to spread out. I saw the table where I had grabbed my drink from earlier, and the castle became visible in the distance. I was almost there.

Almost.

"You look like you're in a hurry," a male voice said from in front of me. My sight was blurred from unreleased tears.

"Leave me alone," I mumbled as I shoved passed him, keeping my head down.

He grabbed my arm and spun me around, forcing me to face him. He was a large fae, almost as tall as Malachi. He had blood-red hair and massive silver wings that tucked tightly behind his shoulders.

And he was looking at me like he had just found exactly what he had been looking for.

"That's no way to talk to a friend," he sneered.

"We aren't friends," I replied coldly.

He looked me up and down slowly, sending a chill down my spine. "Human," he stated. "Interesting. What are you doing out here with all of these fae?" he asked. "It's dangerous, you know."

"I was just leaving," I said. I lifted my chin and looked him straight in his eye.

"Great," he smiled. "Me, too."

Panic erupted through my body. The realization of exactly where I was and what I was doing began to set in. I was one of the three humans in this kingdom right now.

Nobody was coming to help me.

The man's grip on my arm tightened as he turned to begin walking toward the castle.

"Jade," a familiar voice said. *Lucien's voice.* "Everything okay?"

Relief and panic both swarmed me.

He walked up behind me and placed a protective hand on my shoulder. The other fae dropped his grip on my arm immediately.

I wanted to answer, I wanted to tell him to run, to help me. That I was far from okay.

But no words came out.

"We're just fine, thank you," the other fae said.

"She's with me," Lucien replied in a powerful voice. "I suggest you get lost."

It could have still been the effects from the fae drink, or perhaps the cool breeze of the night, but a chill ran down my spine.

The male in front of us eyed Lucien, likely noting his foreign appearance, and shook his head.

"Fine," he said. "But if you're looking for some real fun tonight," he said to me, "come find me."

I didn't exhale until he was out of sight.

Tears streamed down my face as I stood there, focusing on taking one breath after another.

"Saints, Jade. What was that? What are you doing?"

Lucien asked. He moved to face me, but his demeanor changed entirely when he saw the tears.

"I'm fine," I insisted before he could ask any questions.

The words didn't even sound believable. I was the furthest thing from fine. I noted that I would not be drinking any fae drinks again for the entirety of my life. My emotions spiraled.

How could Malachi look at me that way? Like I was a stupid child he felt sorry for. Like he had been doing me a favor this entire time by pretending to be interested in me.

I shook my head.

How damn dumb I had been, believing that he wanted anything to do with me aside from his political aspirations.

I was simply a piece in a larger game. I had forgotten that.

I wouldn't forget again.

"You're not fine, Jade. What happened? Why was that man following you?"

Isaiah approached behind Lucien. "What's going on?" he asked.

Great. An audience.

"Why do you even care?" I asked Lucien. "You were the one ready to torture me not too long ago."

He drew his brows together. "Things have changed since then, Jade. If you want me to rip that guy's head off, I will. Or better yet, I'll tell Malachi what just happened."

"Don't!" I yelled. "Let's just drop this, please," I begged.

"Fine," Lucien said before turning to Isaiah. "Stay with her," he said. "It's not safe for her out here alone."

Isaiah nodded, and Lucien slipped away into the crowd.

"Why was that man talking to you? Was he following you?" Isaiah asked.

"Because I'm human!" I responded, likely a bit too harsh. "I'm a stupid, fragile human, same as you, Isaiah. If any male here wanted to do anything with me, there would be nothing I could do to stop it. So I don't know why he was following me, but I think I could guess."

Isaiah stiffened. "Is that why you're crying?" he asked. "Did he hurt you?"

I laughed. "No, he didn't touch me."

I didn't say any more. I didn't need to. Isaiah glanced back to the crowd, then back to me. "Fae take anything they want, Jade. They always have, and they always will. It's why we need to be smart about this."

"About what?"

"About business. About what they want from us."

How ridiculous. "They don't want anything from us," I replied. "That's the problem."

Isaiah stepped forward. "We have something that they want, Jade."

"Really?" I asked. "And what's that?"

He stared into my eyes, deeply enough that I thought I almost looked away. "We have you."

I took a step back. I don't know where I was heading, but my heart was pounding in my chest. So harshly that I thought it might jump out.

"He's right," Esther's cool, collected voice made me jump.

She approached us from the shadows. How long had she been listening? How long had she been at this festival?

"What does that even mean?" I asked.

"They know what you are now, Jade. And now that you're eighteen, more people will come looking for you."

They cornered me now, backing me up against the wall of the building.

"So what?" I spat. More tears came. My throat burned. "I'm just supposed to hide forever?"

"No, not hide, Jade. Let me teach you who you are. Let me show you what you can do."

"We can't run from them," I said. Esther had to know it. Isaiah had to know it. If the fae wanted to find me, they would.

"You won't have to. They know you as Malachi's wife right now, Jade. We just need time to develop your gifts. We just need something temporary."

My vision blurred.

"Come back to Fearford with us. You're safe there," Isaiah suggested.

"Malachi would never leave me," I spat. "He would never leave me alone."

Why was I defensive? Malachi didn't want me tonight, why would that change?

If Esther was right...

"It's only temporary," Esther said. "Malachi will be on board with anything that keeps you safe."

"And living in Fearford is supposed to help? The King already knows I'm there. That's the first place he'll look."

"We won't have to worry about the King much longer," Isaiah chimed in.

My brain was spinning. Were they saying what I thought they were saying?

"I can't do this right now," I insisted. "I can't... I need..."

Malachi. I needed to talk to Malachi.

"Look," Esther said. "It's been a long night. You have a lot to think about. You're eighteen now, Jade. You're going to start changing very soon. Come find me in the morning, and we'll talk it over. There's no need to make rash decisions just yet."

I took a long, shaky breath. "I have to go," was all I could say.

"Jade, wait," Isaiah yelled at me.

I paused and looked over my shoulder.

"Is Sadie with you?" he asked.

The hair on my neck stood up. "No," I replied. "Why? Where is she?"

Isaiah's eyes widened.

And that's when we heard Sadie's blood-curdling scream.

CHAPTER 17
Jade

The three of us sprinted into the castle, following the sound of Sadie's voice.

"Sadie!" I yelled. "Sadie, where are you?"

"Jade!" she yelled back before her voice was cut off abruptly.

Isaiah's boots hit the ground running in the direction it came from, and he didn't even test to see if the door to the room was unlocked before he kicked it down.

Esther and I followed tightly behind him.

And then we saw him. The same fae that had cornered me just a few minutes ago.

He had Sadie pinned to the wall, looking absolutely terrified.

"What in the–" he started, turning toward us and letting go of Sadie.

His eyes scanned the three of us before ultimately falling onto me.

His bewildered look turned into a smile. "Ah," he said. "It looks like you took me up on my offer after all."

"Stop right there," Esther said behind me. "Or you will regret it. Leave us and get back to the party."

"And who are you, exactly?" he spat. "Another human? Tell me, what do you plan to do to stop me?"

Esther held out her hand and chanted something in a language I couldn't understand.

I could barely process what I was seeing.

The fae's eyes widened before he staggered backward. "What are you?" he whispered. He was already looking at the door, looking for a way out.

Esther didn't stop. She stepped forward, eyes darkening as she continued to chant.

The man didn't say another word.

Isaiah and I backed up enough so he could run out the door as he screamed in pain, and then it was over.

"Sadie," Isaiah said as he rushed to her side. "Sadie, are you okay?"

Sadie had tears streaming down her face. A knot formed in my stomach. Someone as strong as Sadie had to endure a lot to get to this point.

"Get her out of here," Esther ordered. "Take her to the infirmary where she'll be safe."

Isaiah didn't hesitate. He picked Sadie up and left, carrying her further into the castle.

My heart pounded in my ears.

"What the Saints was that?" I asked Esther. "What did you do to him?"

"Nothing you can't learn how to do, also."

I shook my head. "No, that was...that was magic, right?"

Esther nodded. "These fae see themselves as above us, Jade. You are the peacemaker. You are the one that will show them their rightful place."

My breath was shallow. "That fae...he would've..."

"But he didn't," she interrupted. "Because there are people like us to stop him. This is why they need us, Jade. This power imbalance is unjust. Do you understand me?" she asked.

"Yes," I gasped. "Yes, I understand."

"Good," she said. "Now get out of here and go straight to your room. Sadie is fine, everything is okay. Understand?"

I nodded one more time and turned toward my room.

Esther wanted me to be a protector. A *peacemaker*. But if tonight proved anything, it was that Malachi was right.

The fae and the humans were never going to be equals.

CHAPTER 18
Jade

The rest of the bed was empty when I woke up. The afternoon sun blazed through the open window, and *Saints*.

My head was pounding.

I groaned as I threw back the thick sheets, still in the dress I had worn the night before,

My eyes burned, likely from the tears I remembered running down my face for the majority of the night.

I had effectively embarrassed myself, that much was certain.

I silently hoped that everyone else would forget the entire thing.

And Malachi.

I shook my head, trying to forget the entire thing. He didn't matter. Anything I thought I had felt for him didn't matter.

Looking out the window, I saw the sun was nearly to the center of the sky.

I had to find Esther.

I rinsed off the evidence from the night before, tossing the flowered gown to the side and throwing on my comfortable trousers and tunic. I slipped on my leather boots and headed for the door, not even bothering to attempt fixing my hair.

Nobody waited for me outside my door. Nobody guarded me. Nobody was there to ask me where I was going.

At least I had *some* freedom.

I should be grateful for that, at least. Sadie and Isaiah were probably still hiding in the infirmary.

I turned to shut my door and saw there was a note attached to it.

"Jade," it said. *"Come find me when you wake up. Down the hall and to the left."*

I shoved the note in my pocket and headed in that direction.

It had to have been from Esther.

She had been meaning to talk to me, and after what she told me last night, we had a lot to discuss.

Saints. Why hadn't I taken her more seriously? She talked on and on about this prophecy and about how I had to be protected, and I had never questioned it. I had never questioned her.

The truth was, if this prophecy was important enough to her that she would leave her only son in the hands of the monstrous king, it had to be important. It was worth something.

And if Esther was right, now that I was eighteen, things were going to be changing for me. And soon.

It was in my best interest to find out.

The instructions of the note brought me to a large, open room.

"Good," Esther greeted me. "You're here."

"You wanted to talk to me?" I asked.

Esther just nodded, looking me up and down as if she had never seen me before.

My annoyance spiked.

"How are you feeling today?" she asked me.

"I feel fine," I lied. "Thank you for asking, Esther. That's very kind."

Esther eyed me and my sarcasm for a second longer and smirked.

It struck me then how similar she looked to Malachi. She really *was* his mother.

"Fae wine will do you no good in the future, child. If you were smart you would avoid it next time."

"I never claimed to be smart."

"And that's where I think you're lying," she said. "Follow me. I'm taking you somewhere."

She began walking before I could even follow.

I took double the amount of steps to keep up. "Where are we going?"

"To train you."

"Train me for what?"

"For the war that's coming," she said in a calmness that made my blood curdle.

"What war?"

She stopped walking long enough to turn and answer me. "The war we've all been waiting on, sweetheart. The war you're going to win for us."

"How am I going to help you win any war? I'm human, if you forgot."

"Trust me, I will never forget. But that may not be the case for long."

"What's that supposed to mean?"

Esther just continued walking. We walked out of the castle and down a small path that led to a large, open field away from the rest of Trithen. We walked and we walked, until we approached the massive wall that was keeping us separated from whatever evil creatures that lurked beyond.

And then I followed Esther as she led us through a tiny, hidden door in the stone wall.

"We aren't supposed to be out here, Esther. It's dangerous."

"Not for a witch, it's not."

I rolled my eyes. *Great.*

Trusting Esther was an uncertainty. She had saved our lives, but her intentions were still unclear. The prophecy was just that, a prophecy. I had yet to understand her part in all of this. What she wanted from all of us.

Vengeance, perhaps? Did she want the King to die just as badly as the rest of us?

Or perhaps she had made some sort of deal with the Saints.

Time would tell.

We walked into the tree line, far enough that the blazing sun was now covered by the towering trees.

"If we're attacked by a deadling and killed, Malachi won't be happy with you."

"That's a bit of an understatement, princess," Malachi's voice interrupted from behind a tree, causing me to jump.

"Saints! What are you doing here?" I asked.

"Training. Same as you," he answered with a smug look on his face.

I glanced at Esther, who only shrugged. "We had to get out of the castle," she said. "Too many prying ears."

"This can't be good," I mumbled, waiting for an explanation.

"If what my mother believes is correct, you'll begin forming certain... *gifts* now that you are eighteen."

I scoffed. "And nobody has thought about how ridiculous that sounds?"

"It's not ridiculous at all," Esther said. "In fact, the idea that you may not believe in your destiny is the most ridiculous part of all of this."

I shut my mouth.

I was absolutely certain that if I had some sort of magical powers, I would be aware of them. But I was also absolutely certain that Esther had no doubt as to who I was.

And after what happened last night, I owed it to Sadie to at least try and learn if I had any power.

I owed it to myself.

"Okay," I said after a while. "What do you want me to do?"

Esther stepped forward. "There are many forms of *gifts* in this world, child. There are the low-level mages, who are able to bend the elements. Air, fire, water, earth. They're common in the southern regions, and are more or less harmless.

"There are fae, of course, who are randomly gifted certain powers as the Saints allow it. Typically, they aren't as strong as Malachi's gifts. They have magic that can read minds, control air, things like that."

"Fae can read minds?" I interrupted.

"No," she laughed. "It's been decades since I've met another fae with a gift. They're becoming more and more rare, just like witches with natural power."

"Witches? Like you?"

Esther nodded. "Witches used to be the most powerful creatures that walked this earth. You heard what I said about witches needing sacrifices now, but it didn't used to be this way. Witches had free access to power, able to use as much as they needed to, whenever they wanted. That's changed now.

"Then there are the elites. Fae-born children who have been granted gifts much more than that."

"Like Malachi?" I asked, not looking at him.

Esther nodded. "Like Malachi. As you have no doubt seen with your own eyes, Malachi possesses an extraordinary gift. With a single thought, he can inflict crippling pain or even death on anyone he wishes."

From the corner of my eye, I saw Malachi's jaw tighten.

"Do other fae have his gift?"

"None that we have seen, although it wouldn't be impossible."

"And his wings? That's why they're black, isn't it? You're an elite?"

"Those are just titles," Malachi suggested. "It was purely a coincidence that I ended up with this gift. The black wings are a coincidence as well. A mistake by the creator."

"There are no coincidences," Esther spat. "And the creator makes no mistakes."

"What about you?" I asked her. "What type of magic do you possess?"

Esther smiled. "I've been practicing for decades, child. Long before you were ever born. My ancestors once wielded the most powerful magic known to any kingdom. That has long since passed, of course, but their blood still flows in mine."

I waited for her to answer.

"Over the last few decades, I have been known to perform each kind of magic."

Impossible.

"But unlike Malachi and others who were born with their gifts, I must pay a price. Magic does not come free to those who were not chosen for it."

"And you weren't chosen?"

Something flashed across Esther's face, but it

quickly passed. "For some things, I was. Like delivering you for your purpose."

Now we were getting to the fun part. The part I had ignored for much too long. "And what, exactly, is my purpose in this war you say is coming?"

Malachi stepped forward, like he was ready to intercept at any second. "Esther," he warned. "Don't."

"No," I insisted. "I deserve to know. You have all been treating me like a child, talking in code and whispering to each other in the darkness. If I'm to be the tool for this grand plan of yours, I should know what my part is. I deserve at least that."

"She's right," Esther started. "She deserves to know."

Malachi took a long, pained breath. "Fine," he said. He then turned to face me, looking me in the eyes for the first time since last night. "But remember this is just a prophecy, Jade. We can take this one piece at a time."

I braced myself for the next words.

Esther grabbed both of my wrists in hers. Malachi stepped back, but stayed close. "You are the key to everything, Jade. Your mother knew it, too."

"My mother?"

She nodded. "Your mother and I were great friends. You remind me a lot of her, actually. She was stubborn and bratty just like you."

My breath hitched. "How? How did you know her?"

Esther smiled. "Your mother was a part of my clan, darling."

I fought to keep my reactions together. "You mean my mother was a witch?"

"If you want to stick to all these titles, yes. She was."

"Does that mean I..."

"No," she answered quickly. "Not exactly. You see, your mother was a practicing witch, but it was her blood that made you special. You're the one we've been waiting for. Not her."

"Why me? Why not her?"

"It wasn't time, child. Each generation of your family's blood has been waiting for this time in history."

"And what time is that?"

"The time when we needed you the most, Jade."

"I can't save anyone," I muttered. "I...I can't. I can barely keep myself alive, much less entire kingdoms of people. Of fae!"

"We have time, Jade," Esther said. "We have time to develop your magic into something deadly. Something powerful."

I shook my head and pulled my arms from Esther's grasp. "What magic?" I said.

"Come sit," Esther commanded.

I did as I was told, taking a seat on the cool ground of the outdoors. "Now I want you to lay back, all the way."

Again, I obeyed. Malachi stayed where he stood, arms crossed, watching my every movement with furrowed brows.

"Good," she continued. "Now close your eyes, and take three deep breaths."

"I don't see how this is helping anything," I said.

"Just do it."

I did. I closed my eyes and breathed deeply, letting the cool air of the trees refresh my lungs. I held my breath for a second or two before releasing, letting my entire body relax with it.

"Now picture your body connecting to something, like the stem of a flower, diving deep into the ground below you. Picture yourself as one with the earth. As one with the divine being of nature."

I followed her instructions, picturing my body connecting to the vastness of the ground below me. It was relaxing, I had to admit. I felt energized yet blissful at the same time, like I was right where I belonged.

"Now picture the air above you the same way. Imagine the air around you as an extension of your own being. Connected to you. Blessed by you."

I did.

"Feel that energy within you, Jade. Funnel it at your core, right where your heart lies. Make it part of you. Own it."

I tried to follow her instructions, but I still felt no magic. No powers of any sort.

"You aren't being patient," Esther spat. "You have to relax, Jade. Trust that your magic will come to you when you are ready."

"And who says I'm ready?"

"Your husband, for one."

I snapped my eyes open and propped myself on an elbow, glaring at Malachi, who was staring at me with an idiotic smirk on his face.

"Is this funny to you?" I asked. "Me humiliating myself on the ground?"

He didn't answer. Only smiled wider.

Holy Saints.

"Okay," Esther interrupted. "Perhaps we should try something else today. You clearly feel a lot of anger, and magic has a direct tie with emotions. So, let's try that."

"Try what?" I asked. "Being angry? Trust me, it hasn't given me any magical powers yet."

"But it will, Jade," Esther said. "You just have to focus your anger in the right direction."

"Great," Malachi mumbled. "Just what we need."

"Excuse me?"

"Let's start here," Esther interrupted. "Jade, tell us all the things that make you angry about Malachi. And focus on the feelings that come with them."

"You can't be serious," Malachi said.

"Oh, I'm very serious, son. I'll do anything to activate Jade's gifts, and you should feel the same way."

He huffed and crossed his arms again, leaning against the tree as if he couldn't care less what I thought of him.

I stood from the ground and brushed the dirt from my legs before I began.

"First off," I started. "I think he's arrogant. He walks around here like he's to be worshiped. He knows he can kill anyone here, and it goes straight to his head."

"Good," Esther said. "Keep going."

"He's stubborn. He won't listen to anything I tell him. He thinks he is the only one in an entire room full of people who can have a good idea, and it's absolutely absurd."

Malachi stared at me, amusement still twinkling in his eyes. "And he uses people. He used me. He made me think he actually cared about me, when the entire time I was just part of this greater plan of his. I knew it, too. I just let myself believe the other story. The better story."

"What else?" Esther pressed.

Malachi shifted uncomfortably. I had struck a nerve.

Good. He deserved it.

"He's selfish." He rolled his eyes again but returned his gaze to me. "He's the reason my family hates me. He took me from the only person I love. He's the reason the humans don't accept me. He's the reason I can't have a normal life with a normal man who will keep me safe."

A twig snapped in the distance.

The air shifted, and the hair on my neck stood up. Every part of me became alert, even a part of me deep down that seemed to want an awakening.

We weren't alone out here.

CHAPTER 19
Malachi

"D on't move," I whispered. "Stay quiet."

Jade stayed still, but her eyes widened enough to let me know that she heard it, too.

Someone else was out there. Someone or something.

Esther slowly picked up a foot and moved toward me, careful not to crack even the smallest twig.

She had been living comfortably in the forest. She would know how to help me protect Jade.

I reached for the sword strapped to my hip, but didn't unsheathe it.

The slightest sound would give away our location in a heartbeat.

Esther met my eyes and mouthed the word that made my blood run cold:

Deadlings.

I had dealt with deadlings many times in my life, and I had never left with so much as a scratch.

But that was never while I was with a human. Or a witch, for that matter.

I waved my hand to Jade, motioning for her to kneel down. She did, moving as slow as humanly possible.

Another grunt came from my left.

Saints.

There was a small group of them, at least four.

Killing them would be easy. As long as I got to them before any one of them got to Jade.

Esther held a small dagger tightly in her hand. If we made it out of here alive, I would be teaching Jade how to defend herself.

Successfully this time.

My power rumbled in my chest, but I knew it was no use. Because the deadlings were already, well, *dead*, my magic was no use on them. It was almost as if it passed straight through.

"What is it?" Jade whispered through the silence.

Not even one second later, a blood-curdling shriek split the air.

I couldn't move fast enough. A black figure, one of those disgusting deadlings, shot out of nowhere and tackled Jade. She screamed, and I lunged after her with my sword out.

They tumbled on the ground, Jade barely keeping her face away from its snapping jaws as it clawed its way toward her.

"Jade!" I yelled as I closed the gap between us. I held my sword out, but she was moving too much. One wrong move would be deadly. My heart stopped as she screamed again, the monster's claws digging into her skin.

I didn't hesitate this time. One swift motion, and the creature's head rolled to the ground with a thud.

I had no time to make sure she was okay. I spun on my heel, turning to where Esther fought off another deadling behind me.

They had each other by the shoulders, Esther backing up as the disgusting death overpowered her.

I grabbed the thing by the back of the head and threw. Hard. Its crunchy body smacked a tree a few feet away and fell to the ground.

Two more appeared from the trees. Coming directly at us.

Jade was still on the ground behind me.

"Protect her," I ordered Esther as I stepped in front of them both. Esther moved to guard Jade, dagger in hand. Esther may not have been strong enough to kill one with her bare hands, but she at least stood a chance.

I dropped the two other deadlings in an instant, my sword hitting true and slicing through the bodies with little effort.

"Saints," Jade breathed behind me.

I turned to see what she was talking about.

And blistering pain erupted in my shoulder.

I elbowed the creature that bit me, a sickening crack filling the air around us.

Adrenaline pulsed through my body, my power was begging to help me. But I knew it couldn't. With one arm, I raised my sword and cut the deadling in half.

Its body hit the ground with a thud.

And then...

Silence.

Our panting breaths were the only sounds in the forest.

We stayed there like that for a few minutes, trying to understand what had just happened. Processing it.

"Son," Esther said after a while. "Your arm."

I glanced down to where I had been bitten.

Red and black blood dripped down past my elbow. It stung like a bitch, I had to admit.

"Malachi," Jade whispered. She rushed past Esther and held her hands out like she was going to touch it, but changed her mind at the last second.

"It's fine," I whispered. "Nothing I can't handle."

"What will happen?" she asked. "What happens if you are bit by one of those things?"

"If I were a human?" I responded. "I would probably die."

Jade's eyes widened, just for a split second, before she rolled them at me. "I'm being serious, Malachi. You're not going to turn into one of those things are you?"

I nearly laughed at how concerned she was. "No, I won't. Although I have to admit that would be pretty fun."

"There will be more nearby," Esther interrupted. "They must have sensed we were here."

"Like they were hunting us?" Jade asked. "Do they have that ability?"

"Deadlings are killers. If they scent anything they can sink their teeth into, they'll stop at nothing until they get to it."

"Even fae?"

"Even fae."

Jade shook her head. "Then why in the Saints did we come out here? We could have done this in the cozy safety of those massive walls!"

Esther raised her hand. "Just because the leaders of Trithen have invited us here doesn't mean we are able to trust them fully. You are too trusting, child. You have to be more vigilant."

Jade put a hand on her hip and scoffed. "I'm the one that's too trusting? As if you two didn't just drag us out here into danger, with who knows how many other random creatures that want to eat us!"

I covered my mouth with my fist, but couldn't stop the laugh that erupted from my mouth.

"What?" she half-yelled at me. "Is something funny about us almost dying?"

"No, nothing at all," I responded.

"Good," she responded. "I'm glad you find amusement in all of this, Malachi. I think we've had enough training for one day." She turned toward the castle and started storming away.

"We'll have to train every day," Esther added. "Every day until your powers begin to develop."

"Whatever," Jade spat.

Esther gave me a knowing look. "Go," she mouthed.

I rolled my eyes and jogged to catch up to Jade.

"Jade," I said. "Wait."

"No thanks."

"Jade, I'm sorry," I said. I *was* sorry. Everything that I had said to her last night... she needed to hear it. It was going to keep her safe, especially while I plotted to kill my own father. But there would have been a better time and place to tell her those things.

And just because it was a terrible idea to be together didn't mean I didn't want it more than anything in the world.

Jade just laughed flatly and kept walking.

"Fine," I continued. "If you don't want to talk to me, you can at least listen. I'll oversee training you aside from magic work with Esther. Whatever drama is happening between us is going to have to wait until this is figured out."

Jade shook her head, her messy black hair bouncing with every step. At least she was listening to me.

"I don't want to train," she said. "Not with you."

The hatred in her voice made me inhale sharply, but it was my own fault. Her pain was because of me. I deserved that.

"I'll see you in the morning," I said anyway. "Meet me here at sunrise."

CHAPTER 20
Jade

It couldn't be more clear that Malachi didn't want me. I had been a mere tool to him this entire time.

I cursed at myself in the darkness of the empty bedroom. He wouldn't even sleep in the same room as me? I was his *wife*.

There had been a time when I thought I wouldn't be able to keep him out of my bedroom.

Saints, had I been wrong.

I rolled over and stared at the moonlight blaring into the window. I likely only had a few hours of darkness left, then I had to meet him for more training.

For more embarrassment.

But we had to work together. I had to stay alive, and if war was coming, Malachi *would* be my best teacher.

I wanted to learn how to fight. I needed to learn how to defend myself.

I stared at the ceiling, my body buzzed with adrenaline just thinking about fighting.

I had been able to defend myself against humans most of the time. I had enough practice with that back home, anyway. But taking on fae was an entirely different battle.

And now there was a target on my back.

I peeled back my silk sheets and crawled out of the bed. I was too antsy to sleep. Rest wasn't coming anytime soon.

I had to do something.

I slipped a robe over my thin nightgown and inched my door open slowly.

The library was nearby, maybe I would head there. Or head back outside for some extra practice on whatever magic tricks Esther was trying to teach me.

A woman's laughter caught my attention. I tiptoed closer in the direction it was coming from. Not because I cared, really. Moreso because my curiosity had gotten the best of me.

Who was awake at this hour, anyway?

Besides me, of course.

I wrapped my arms around my body in the chill of night as I peeked my head around the corner.

I had to squint my eyes to see in the darkness, but as soon as they adjusted, I regretted ever leaving my room.

Adeline was sitting in the middle of a large study, kicking her feet and laughing in the darkness.

Only she wasn't alone.

I could have spotted that dark hair anywhere. Serefin and her were together, with their arms wrapped around one another and their bodies tangled together in the darkness.

I pushed myself off the wall and back into the shadows as fast as possible.

I wasn't sure why I was the one who felt like I was doing something wrong. They were the ones *making out* in the middle of the night.

Saints. I wanted to laugh. I wanted to run and tell Tessa, the only person I knew besides Adeline who ever cared for stupid drama like that.

But instead, I covered my mouth with my own hand in the darkness until my breathing settled, and tried to make my way back to my room.

Only when I turned to head back the direction I had come, I tripped on the long skirt of my nightgown. I slapped my hand against the stone wall to catch myself, which was anything but silent.

"Did you hear that?" Serefin's protective voice boomed through the empty study.

Adeline just giggled again. "Hear what?" she cooed.

"Someone's out there."

"There's no one here," Adeline continued. "You're being paranoid."

I pressed my back into the wall, as if hiding against it would save me.

But footsteps came closer and closer. I couldn't move. I couldn't hide. There was nowhere to go.

Serefin rounded the corner like a man chasing something.

Yet he stopped dead in his tracks as soon as his eyes met mine.

"I– I was just..." I stuttered.

Serefin shook his head. "No, I mean I–"

We both stared at each other, completely blank.

Until Adeline rounded the corner. "Saints, Ser! You scared me! It's just Jade!"

She tossed her head back and took a deep breath.

"What are you two doing out here in the middle of the night?" I asked. Even though I already knew the answer.

Serefin batted his eyes. "Nothing," he answered in a heartbeat.

Adeline and I both just stared at him.

"Look," she stepped in. "We don't want Malachi to know. I'm his sister and Ser is his best friend. It would just be weird."

"What exactly are you hiding from him? Are you two..."

"We're just hanging out," she replied. "That's all."

"Right. That's what it looked like in there."

Adeline and Serefin looked at each other, then back at me. I spoke next. "Look, if you don't want me to tell Mal, I won't. Whatever this is, it's none of my business. It's not like he even talks to me anymore anyway."

"Oh, please," Adeline spat. "You two are head over heels for each other. It won't be long until we're redoing the wedding just so he can declare his love for you."

I blushed in the darkness.

"I'll leave you two to it then," I whispered. I turned on my heel and started back down the hallway.

"Thank you, Jade!" she called after me. I held up a hand and waved back, not daring to turn back around.

I got back to my room and stayed there until the morning sun began peaking back through the glass window.

"Let's go," was all Malachi managed to say to me as he brushed past me in the garden, storming into the vast field of Trithen.

"Good morning to you, too."

"We don't have much time before the others meet us. I'll have to train you twice as hard to get caught up with the others. We have a few weeks before you need to be ready, but it took most of these soldiers decades to be able to fight off a trained fae."

"Great, lovely pep talk."

His eyes darkened. "This isn't a laughing matter, Jade. Your life is on the line."

"That is nothing new to me."

Malachi eyed me for a second, challenging me.

I didn't budge.

I had spent the last few hours of the night thinking

of all the things I would say to him. I pictured how great it would feel to yell at him. To scream. To tell him how incredibly shitty it felt to be in my position right now, a mere human used as a pawn by the entire fae kingdom.

But nothing would do this justice. Nothing would be good enough.

I sauntered after him, walking deeper and deeper into the field until the only thing I could see around us was knee-high grasses.

"Okay," Malachi announced, surveying the surrounding area and nodding as if he had decided the spot was good enough for our training.

I stopped beside him.

"Now run back to the castle," he said.

Did he just say...

"Excuse me?" I asked. He did not just say that.

Malachi only nodded. "We'll start with endurance training. You aren't strong enough to fight a fae just yet, but you should damn well be able to run away from one if you need to. Get moving."

I clenched my jaw, but arguing would only satisfy him. I knew he was doing this to piss me off. He knew I wanted to train, wanted to learn to defend myself. He had known that since before we ever left Rewyth.

I guess today wasn't going to be the day for that.

So, I turned back toward the castle, which was now barely a blip in the distance, and I started to jog.

Jogging was nothing new to me. I used to run to

the market and back at home, sometimes out of boredom.

It's not that I was particularly out of shape. I just hadn't moved much in the few weeks that I had been married off.

And there was a long way back to the castle.

"Tired already?" Malachi's taunting voice. "You'll have to be faster than that, princess."

I couldn't respond. My mouth was occupied by the heavy breaths as I panted with every step.

Saints. I was pathetic.

But I didn't stop. There was no way I was going to give him that satisfaction. There was no way he was going to get the better of me on our first day of training.

Sweat began to bead on my skin. The morning sun was fully visible now, blaring down on us with not a single cloud for shade.

I put one foot in front of the other again. And again. And again. Until Malachi's taunting wasn't even in my mind. Until the only thing I was focused on was that castle getting closer and closer and closer.

And we eventually made it.

"Not bad," he breathed behind me when we made it. He was hardly even out of breath, meanwhile I couldn't even waste enough breath to talk.

I nodded and knelt over, placing a hand on each knee while I caught my breath.

"Now do it again," he demanded. I didn't even have

time to catch my breath before Malachi was insisting I move forward, running all the way back to the field.

But wasting my breath arguing wouldn't help me. I bit my tongue and started moving back to the field, even as my lungs screamed for me to stop.

We spent the next couple of hours doing the same thing. Malachi demanded. I obeyed every command. I didn't catch my breath once. Not one single time. Yet I continued doing everything Malachi demanded of me.

Sweat drenched my clothes. Even the linens I had worn were completely soaked, my top clinging to my damp skin.

"Take a break," he said to me. "The others should be joining us soon."

"The others?" I breathed.

"You thought you were the only one I was training?" he asked. "In case you forgot, sweetheart, I'm one of the most powerful fae in this kingdom. I've fought wars these men have only heard about in rumors. Seth asked me to train them, and I agreed."

I was exhausted, yes, but this still didn't make much sense. "What do you mean he asked you? Is that what we're doing here then? Training his men?"

Malachi nodded but wouldn't look me in the eye. "For the most part, yeah."

"And then what?"

"What do you mean?"

"You train his men, and then what? What are you training them for?"

Malachi exhaled and placed his hands on his hips, like he was finally tired.

A familiar sensation hit my stomach. "What?" I asked again. "Just tell me already."

"It's my father," he said.

"What about him?"

"Seth wants me to kill him."

CHAPTER 21
Malachi

"I really hope you were planning on telling me that sometime soon," Jade snapped.

"Why? It's not like it involves you," I retorted. I didn't care that I sounded harsh. I needed to keep her out of this.

"Are you kidding me? You really think that you being on a mission to kill your own father has nothing to do with me? The girl he wants dead?"

I sighed again. What did she want me to say? My brothers and I had already planned to kill him before Seth got involved. Now, we were just doing a small favor.

It was nothing. Simple politics. I needed an ally when shit went down.

This was the clear choice. *Wasn't it?*

Disbelief covered Jade's face. "I was going to tell you," I admitted after a few seconds. Saints. Her sweat had made her shirt nearly see-through.

"So, you're training Trithen, your previous enemies, on how to fight? Am I hearing that correctly?"

"Yes."

"Have you told Esther? Does Isaiah know? What about Adeline?"

"It's nobody else's business, Jade. This is between Seth and I, okay?"

She shook her head and backed up a step. I wanted to reach a hand out, but I stopped myself.

"Serefin knows. I'll tell the others."

"Your mother won't like it."

I laughed. "I don't really care what she thinks, Jade."

"You should. You're about to kill one parent. You might as well keep this one around."

"And why do you suddenly care? You didn't like Esther, remember? You didn't like any of them when we met."

I was yelling now, we both were.

"Yeah well, things change, Malachi!"

"They sure as shit do," I mumbled, turning my back to her. "The others will be here soon."

"Right," I said. "You'll be too busy teaching your enemies all your best fighting tactics to talk to me. Got it."

I spun around on my heel. My mind was spinning, Jade made me crazy. Absolutely nuts. "Why do you even care?" I asked. "Why do you care about what I'm doing, or what our business with Trithen is?"

Her face changed before she said, "You did not just ask me that."

All I did was shrug, even though I wanted to say more. My instincts begged me to say more.

Jade simply nodded, as if she were finally accepting who I was. Who the monster was that she had been forced to marry.

"If you even have to ask me that question, Malachi, then you clearly haven't been paying any attention over the last few weeks."

And with that, she turned toward the castle and stormed off.

"We aren't done with training!" I yelled after her. Saints, I was a dumb ass.

"I don't give a shit!" she yelled back.

Fair enough.

I let her walk away this time. Back to the castle. Back to another prison she was being held in.

Did she even want to stay? Did she want to help? Had she been interested in me because she thought it would help her get home sooner? Or was she starting to like her place at my side?

It didn't matter anymore, anyway. I had ruined it all. I had been a complete asshole to her. Jade didn't care about my reputation or the people I had killed. She cared about me. For whatever odd, insane reason, she actually cared about me.

And I had ruined it all.

"What's going on out here?" Serefin asked as he jogged up. "Jade looked pissed."

"Yeah," I mumbled. "That pretty much sums it up."

"You know, Mal, if you want to keep her safe, you should send her away. Get her out of here before this war goes down."

"We don't even know if there will be a war yet."

Serefin tilted his head and shrugged.

"Okay, fair," I admitted. "But she's safest here with me. I can keep an eye on her here. She has a target on her back now, and she's one of us from now on whether she likes it or not."

"Did you tell her that?" Ser asked.

"Why should I?"

Serefin took a long breath and laughed silently. "Look, Mal. I know you care about her. I knew that from the moment you first saved her life. But Jade doesn't just need you to protect her. Soon enough, if the rumors are true, she'll be able to do that on her own."

I waited for him to continue.

"Jade needs you to be there, idiot. I saw her walking around the castle at nearly three in the morning last night. Have you even tried spending time with her?"

"Why would I? I'll kill my father and she'll go back to her family. It's that simple."

"No," he said firmly. "It's not. Even if the King is dead, Jade will still be targeted. She'll have to fulfill the prophecy or she'll be hunted her whole life."

Shit. Ser was right about that. I hadn't bothered to think that far ahead.

"Pretending to be a real married couple won't help anyone," I said. "She was forced to marry me, remember? She doesn't want any of this."

"Did she tell you that, or is that what you've been telling yourself?"

I eyed Serefin. When did he become so smart? "You know I pay you to kill our enemies, not give me life advice, right?"

He just shrugged. "Consider this a free bonus then, brother," he said.

"And Ser?" I called. "What the Saints were you doing up at three in the morning?"

He smiled slyly and looked down at his feet. "Why don't you ask that wife of yours?"

The look on his face almost made me smile. Serefin wasn't one to smile frequently or laugh at himself. Something was up.

And Jade knew what it was.

"Fine," I admitted. "I'll talk to her."

"It's about damn time," he said back. "You can finally stop taking up the only extra spare room in the entire castle."

I rolled my eyes and shoved him in the arm. Other soldiers were approaching now, and they would expect warrior Malachi.

Killer Malachi.

Not *laughing-with-his-buddy* Malachi. That wasn't the person who won wars. Who ruled kingdoms.

Serefin knew this, too. We both rolled our shoulders back and crossed our arms behind our backs, waiting to greet our new soldiers.

The soldiers we had seen before.

On the other side of the battlefield.

"Gentleman," I greeted. "Welcome."

The crew in front of us looked like survivors, that much was certain. At this point in time, though, any fae over the age of twenty that lived here would have to be. Two decades ago, we had slaughtered nearly three quarters of their army in war.

Including their king.

The soldiers standing before me looked a lot like the soldiers back then. They were tall and mostly blonde. Compared to the people of Rewyth, they were lighter. Softer.

But their eyes were just as dark.

Some wore strips of armor, likely to train and practice for battle.

Others came shirtless, ready to fight with just their bodies.

The field before us filled and filled, soldiers trickling in from every direction.

"Alright," Serefin said, taking over for me. "Who here knows how to fight?"

Most of the men in front of us raised their hands.

Serefin nodded.

"Right, now who wants to tell me why you're all wrong?"

A few slurs were muttered in the crowd.

I knew these soldiers would hate us, especially if any of them recognized me.

And with my black wings, that wasn't going to be hard.

I tucked them a little tighter into my back.

"Traitors!" one of them yelled.

"Kill them!"

"King killer!"

"Who even let them into this kingdom?"

More insults were yelled and slurred from the crowd.

Serefin and I exchanged a glance.

"We came here to train you," I said. "Because, unlike some of you here, I have never fought a war and lost. Never. Can you say the same?"

This time, the crowd was silent.

"Good. Now we can stand here and bicker about the past, or we can get to work. What do you think?"

I thought they would finally listen, but in a flash, a dagger sliced through the air heading straight toward my head.

I dodged it effortlessly.

Gasps rang out around us, but nobody moved.

"I see some of us are not on board with training," I said, looking around the crowd. "So let me be clear. I have been asked by your king to train you for war. You can try to kill me, but you will fail. You can try to throw daggers at my head, but you will fail. Not a single one of you is capable of killing me. Do you know why that is, Serefin?" I asked.

Serefin shrugged dramatically and said, "No, please tell us."

I eyed the men in front of me. They looked smug. They looked defiant. They looked like they didn't listen to a single word I had just said.

That would get them killed. Their arrogance.

My power rumbled, like it already knew what I was thinking. I pictured my magic branching out and brushing everyone as it passed by, just a simple kiss on their skin.

And every single soldier on the field dropped to the ground in pain.

Serefin and I were the only ones left standing as I reeled my power back in, but the soldiers still moaned, some even yelling for the pain to stop even though it already had.

And someone else. Someone else stood in the back of the crowd, unaffected by my magic.

Jade.

My breath escaped me. "Saints," I mumbled. I stormed past the soldiers on the ground, needing to get to her.

Needing to see if I had hurt her.

But she didn't take her eyes off mine as I approached and grabbed her by the shoulders.

"What are you doing?!" I asked. "I could have killed you!"

"I'm here to train," was all she said. "Nice little trick, by the way."

I couldn't believe what I was seeing. My heart still

pounded in my chest, adrenaline pulsing through me. "What do you mean?" I asked, looking her up and down and making sure she wasn't hurt. "You aren't hurt?"

"No, I'm fine," she said, sounding more annoyed than anything. "I'm fine, Malachi."

It was impossible. I had aimed my power at every single person standing in front of me in that field.

Every single person.

Without excluding my wife.

I turned around and looked at Serefin, who looked just as bewildered as I did.

But the other soldiers were starting to stand now, too. And they were not going to be happy. This would have to wait.

"Fine," I said. "But come to the front with me. You shouldn't be around all of these men anyway."

She didn't argue. Just rolled her eyes and followed me back to the front of the crowd.

"Alright men," I announced, shaking off any nerves that lingered. "Now you know who you're really up against. And trust me, that was only a taste."

Nobody replied this time. Nobody yelled anything toward us.

They were finally starting to learn.

"Serefin will lead you in a few combat warm-ups. Listen to him, or you'll get a taste of what this power can really do."

I grabbed Jade's arm and marched off, dragging her with me.

"Mal, stop!" she yelled. "I'm supposed to be training just like everyone else!"

When we were far enough away, I let her go. "Tell me what you did," I said. Her eyes widened, and I could scent the lingering fear in her emotions. The fear she was trying to hide. "Tell me what you did to block my magic. Did Esther teach you that?"

She only shook her head, eyes wide. "I don't know, Mal. I don't-"

"I need you to tell me, Jade. Because you should be dead right now. Saints..."

I paced, running my hands through my hair and trying to make sense of the situation. "Saints, Jade! If a human gets touched by my power...you blocked it somehow. That's the only thing that makes sense."

"I swear I didn't do anything. I was standing there just like everyone else when they all fell to the ground!"

Her teasing voice was gone now. She was dead serious.

"Shit," I said. I turned and headed to the castle. "Come with me."

"Where are we going?" I asked.

"To find Esther and ask her how it's possible that you're even alive right now."

CHAPTER 22
Jade

"It's not impossible that she can block your power," Esther whispered. Malachi had been desperate for answers, and had stormed us directly into Esther's bedroom. "I've heard of this before. An individual able to block the powers of others."

"Are you sure?" Malachi insisted.

"There's one way we can know for sure. Try it again," she said.

"Absolutely not. It's too dangerous."

I pushed myself off the wall and walked toward Mal. "It's not too dangerous," I insisted. "If you could hurt me, you would have done it. In that field. I know you can't hurt me Mal. It's like... it's like an instinct that I can feel. Just try it."

He stared at me, hesitating for a moment. "I don't like this."

"I know you don't."

Silence filled the air. Malachi had been a complete asshole to me recently, but the way he looked at me now made me rethink everything.

He was afraid of hurting me.

"Fine," he said after a few minutes. "I'll try it just this once, but if we're wrong..."

"We aren't," Esther and I said at the same time.

Malachi stepped forward and grabbed me by the shoulders. I pretended not to notice the feeling of warmth on my body where he touched me.

"If you feel anything, I'll stop," he whispered. His eyes darkened, and he looked at me now under those thick eyelashes of his.

"Okay," I tried to say, but it was more of a breath.

Malachi closed his eyes, as if he were focusing more than ever on the power within him.

I wasn't afraid, though. I knew what had happened. I knew that Malachi had sent his power out to hurt every single person in that field, and I was the only one who was unaffected.

It wasn't an accident. I felt it deep inside of me.

A few seconds passed, then Malachi let go of me. "It's true," he whispered to himself. His face had changed from one of doubt and worry to one of utter disbelief. "It's true, you aren't affected by my power."

The smile on his face was contagious. "Saints," I breathed. "What does this mean?"

Malachi ran a hand through his messy, disheveled hair. "I've never seen this before. In the decades that

I've been using my magic, the only creatures my magic doesn't work on is the deadlings."

"That's a confidence boost," I said. My mind began to spin. "What are the deadlings, anyway? Are they born that way? Turned?"

Esther stepped forward to answer, her long, white dressing gown trailing the ground behind her. "They didn't use to be this way," she said. "Centuries ago, the deadlings were their own species. They hunted and killed, but it was purely for survival. Just like the rest of us at the time."

Malachi listened intently, too.

"Somewhere over the years, things changed. Some believe they were cursed by the Saints. That the Saints stopped protecting them."

"Does this mean I can block *any* fae powers?" I asked.

"Most likely, yes. If you can block the power from an elite, you can likely block them all."

"This is good news, right?"

Malachi nodded. "It's a relief, definitely."

Esther began talking again, going on and on about the history of magic blockers and what this could possibly mean for the prophecy, but I wasn't listening. I quit listening entirely. Malachi was staring directly at me, eyes burning into mine. It was like he was finally seeing me for the first time.

Actually seeing me. Not pitying me. Not worrying about me.

Like he really saw me.

I wanted to reach out to him. I wanted to throw my arms around him and not let go. I just wanted him.

Malachi broke eye contact before I did. "Okay," he said. "We better get back to training, then. And Esther, let's agree to keep this between us, yes?"

She nodded, and Malachi left the room. I followed behind.

"Back to training?" I repeated behind him. "You mean you're going to let me train with the rest of them?"

He nodded. "If you have these gifts now, more are surely on their way. You need to learn to protect yourself."

I agreed.

"But I won't go easy on you," he added. "If you want to train like a soldier, you'll be treated like one."

"Fine," I said. "I can do that."

He eyed me, his eyes dragging up and back down my body once, in a way that sent a shiver down my spine. But then he turned and walked outside, back to the field.

Back to training.

Serefin and Malachi led everyone through hours and hours of movements. They were basic, yet for my weak body, they took all the energy I had left. Saints. The day had already been so long.

The sun blazed hotter and hotter with every passing minute.

We watched Serefin and repeated his movements, one after another. Sometimes he would show us movements that involved a sword or a dagger, granted nobody had weapons just yet. We repeated the same motions again and again and again.

And we repeated it all the next day.

And the next day.

Before I knew it, two weeks had passed.

My body ached every single day, but I could tell I was getting stronger. Each motion became a sliver easier every day that I tried again. Serefin's nods of approval kept me going each day, although ridiculous slurs from the fae soldiers were also a decent motivator.

Every so often, I would glance at Malachi. He didn't speak to me. Didn't even give me instruction. But here and there I would look at him only to find him already looking at me.

He never looked away first, either. Just kept staring.

Outside of training, we didn't talk. I didn't see him. He would train me for endurance every single morning, and I was too busy catching my breath every single minute that striking up a useless conversation was not an option.

When it came time to train with the rest of the soldiers, Malachi quit talking to me entirely. His attention was on the crowd. He made a point to shut everyone up if anyone began yelling things toward me, but that was it.

He was all business.

This repeated every day. I thought I had been making progress with Malachi in the mornings, but he was harsher with me every single day. He pushed me further and further, until I thought I would break.

But I never did. Ever.

"Alright," Serefin said. "I think that's enough for the day." Soldiers grunted and nodded all over the field. "Get some sleep, we'll try more tomorrow."

I heard a few mumbling about how we weren't training real skills, not using real weapons, and I nearly laughed. Serefin and Malachi knew what they were doing.

Even I could see that.

The rest of the soldiers were wandering back to the castle, eager to eat dinner after another long day of training.

I lingered behind, though. A certain determination had been growing inside of me every day. I wanted to fight Malachi. I wanted to show him that I wasn't the same, useless human he had known weeks ago.

"Training is over," he mumbled when he noticed I had stayed back. "Go home."

I pulled my dagger from my belt, the one that he had gifted me lifetimes ago, and tossed it into the grass beside me.

It was an invitation for a spar. And he knew it.

He took a long, tired breath and disarmed himself before turning to face me. "Fine," he said. "Show me what you've got, wife."

Malachi did not wait another second. He threw his fist into my torso, but I was ready. I blocked it with my forearm, ignoring the satisfying sting that followed.

"You're stronger now," he admitted. I grunted in response.

"I better be."

I swung a leg out and tried to knock him off balance. He dodged it with ease.

Okay. I had to be smart about this. What had I learned in my training? The fae were fast, but they were predictable. After practicing the same movements time and time again for days on end, I should know his next move.

I stepped forward, acting like I was making a move toward his stomach, and when Malachi moved to advance on me I side-stepped, causing him to stagger forward.

We danced around each other.

He mimicked me, and I knew the wicked smile on my face matched his.

"You really are getting better, princess. I must say I'm impressed."

It was a compliment, but he still underestimated me.

I might have been human, but I wasn't completely useless.

Malachi's wings were tucked tightly behind his back. Wings were the most sensitive part of a fae. If I could get a solid hit...

My thoughts were interrupted when Malachi threw an arm around my waist and tossed me on the ground.

He laughed as I got myself up.

"Still not fast enough, though," he said.

I was angry now.

My face was hot, my muscles were ready. I sent a small fist flying toward his face.

He caught it and pulled my body toward him. "Gotta be better than that, princess."

With my free arm, I moved to elbow his side.

He blocked that, too, then shoved my body away from him.

I barely caught myself from falling to the ground.

He was taunting me.

"Again," he said. His voice boomed. It commanded.

I took two steps toward him and tried again.

And again.

He blocked me each time, and each time he had some sort of comment to add.

"I can't do it," I said after he had put me on my ass for probably the hundredth time. "I'm not strong enough."

"What did you just say?" he said. Something in his voice made me want to shut up, but I repeated myself anyway.

"I said I'm not strong enough."

Malachi tilted his head to the sky and took a deep breath before storming toward me and kneeling in the grass before me.

"Don't say that," he said. "The moment you admit it to yourself, it becomes true. And it's not true, so don't say that. You have to protect yourself, Jade. *You have to.* I won't always be around. And when this is all over and you end up going home..."

He didn't finish the sentence. I didn't say anything.

Malachi was close enough now that I could see the small freckles on his face that had formed in the weeks had spent training under the sun.

He looked good in the sun.

"Okay," I managed to breathe. "I understand."

"Good," he said as he stood up again. "Now try again. This time, don't try to overpower me. It will never work. Try something else. Remember your training."

I took a deep breath and tried to focus. He was right. Overpowering a fae wasn't going to be an option.

I had to be smarter than that. Smarter than him.

I stood up from the grass and got back into my fighting stance. Feet slightly parted, fists up to protect my face.

But that would never work. Not on him.

I dropped my fists and raised my hands over my head, pretending to stretch my sides. "Saints," I said. "I'm just so sore these days, you now? All that training, day after day..."

Malachi dropped his own defenses, and I watched as his gaze flickered down to the sliver of skin that was now exposed at my stomach.

His gaze lingered, and the air between us electrified.

With him distracted, I tried again. I swung a leg toward his shin, and to my surprise, actually landed a hit.

Malachi staggered backward, only a step. It took

him a second to realize what the Saints had just happened.

And when he finally realized it, he looked pissed.

"What was that?" he growled.

"What was what?" I responded innocently. "Just fighting a little smarter, that's all."

Malachi growled and moved before I could even think, tackling me to the ground.

He pinned me there, holding my arms to the ground next to my head. "Do you think this is a joke?" he said.

I didn't back down. "I just did what you asked," I spat. "It's not my fault you were distracted."

Malachi laughed, but it wasn't out of joy. It was a laugh that nearly made me shiver in the heat of the sun.

He was still on top of me, his body directly on top of my torso. I tried to buck my hips, but it was no use.

Malachi bent forward, getting eerily close to my face. "Careful there, Jade. You don't want to give the wrong impression. Tell me, is this how you plan on taking down all of your enemies?"

Did he really just say that?

I frowned and tried to buck even harder. "Get off of me!" I yelled.

Malachi just smiled, and his gaze moved from my eyes down to my lips, then back again.

Was he going to kiss me? My stomach fluttered at the thought, but it left abruptly when he stood and stalked off, leaving me on the ground.

"What in the Saints is your problem?" I yelled after

him. I was pissed off. Who did he think he was, toying me around and then nearly kissing me?

Malachi spun around. "What are you talking about?"

"You're a complete asshole to me for weeks and now this? Saints, Malachi. You're treating me like I'm a damn stranger!"

"No, I'm not," he said quietly.

"Oh really? Then where have you been? What have you been spending all your time doing? Because you sure as shit have not been spending it with me."

"I've been busy, Jade. You know that."

"Really? Ever since the festival?"

"That's what you're mad about? The festival?"

Malachi shook his head in disbelief.

"I'm not mad about the festival. I'm mad that my husband has been treating me like a damn burden on his shoulders!"

"Stop being dramatic," he mumbled. Tears stung my eyes. I fought to keep them back. I wasn't going to let him see me cry. Not now. Not after all this.

"I am your wife, Malachi," I admitted through gritted teeth, barely loud enough to hear.

"I know," he replied just as softly.

"Your wife!"

"I know!"

The silence that came after was more than enough to answer any lingering questions I had.

There was no hope. This was how it was going to be from now on. Malachi acting like he had better things to deal with, and me chasing after the dream that there had ever been anything more between us.

"Do you even want me here?" I asked. "Or is this all just part of the prophecy to you?"

Malachi snapped his attention to me, like he couldn't believe what I had just said. I waited for his response.

With two large steps, he closed the gap between us, grabbing my face with both hands. "No," he said firmly, almost yelling. "This is not just part of the prophecy, Jade. You are my wife, and I–"

Love you.

I wasn't sure why I expected those words, but when they didn't come, a familiar sick feeling sank in my chest.

And just as quickly as he had approached me, he dropped his hands and walked away.

I didn't stop him when he kept walking, leaving me alone in the field.

And I finally let the tears fall.

CHAPTER 23
Malachi

Saints, I was an idiot.

I wanted to kiss Jade. I had come so damn close.

The fact that she still cared about me was a damned miracle to me. After the way I had been treating her, she should hate me. She earned the right to hate me.

But she didn't. That had to mean something, right?

Jade was going to turn into an extremely powerful woman. I could feel it in my bones. Esther could, too. She made that very clear a couple of weeks ago.

Jade being able to block my magic didn't change anything. She was still in incredible danger.

If anything, she was in even more danger now.

Being with me would put yet another target on her back.

"We need to talk," Seth approached me as I walked through the castle walls toward the dining room.

"About?"

"Your father is coming here. It's time."

Saints. Was everyone in this place losing their damn minds?

"My father is coming here?" I repeated. I had to make sure I heard him correctly before letting panic take hold.

Seth nodded. "He says he has a new business proposition."

"Could it be because he somehow figured out that we were here?"

Seth shook his head. "It's impossible. Trithen has no spies. I know every single person that comes in and out of these walls, and they're all to be trusted."

Just as ignorant as I thought he was, then.

I sighed and continued walking. "Did you hear me?" he called after me. "We need to prepare!"

"We are prepared," I said. "I'll keep my side of the deal, don't worry."

"You sure you'll be able to do it?" he asked.

My wings flared out by my sides. "What did you just ask me?"

"I just want to be sure."

"It'll get done," was all I could say back.

"Fine," he said. "He will be here tomorrow. You should prepare yourself."

I didn't look back as I stormed into the dining hall.

A few people looked my way as I walked into the room, but I kept my head down. If anyone approached me right now, I would have absolutely no problem punching them in the face.

I walked directly to the servant's table and grabbed food for myself.

A fight was coming, that much was certain.

My father was on his way here...

If he knew I was here, he would bring an entire army. Being here with the leader of Trithen was certainly treason in Rewyth. We had been enemies for too long.

There was too much at risk.

I had to find my brothers.

"**A**nd you think this will work?" Isaiah asked.

I looked at Lucien and Adonis, who sat across the large table. "It has to," Adonis answered. "This might be our only opportunity to kill him."

I nodded. "If anything happens..."

"It won't," Lucien spat. "We'll kill the bastard and it'll be done. Then we can all go home."

He was right. He had to be right.

The twins, Eli and Fynn, sat silently in the back of the room. I hadn't heard them this silent since... ever.

"Everything sound good to you two?" I asked them. They nodded in unison.

It had to be nerves. They had never been put into a fight like this. Had never gone to war.

Shit. They had likely never actually killed anyone.

"What about the soldiers you've been training?" Adonis asked. "Won't they want to know the plan?"

I clenched my jaw. "We can't trust them. I killed their king. I don't know what their game is here, but we can't assume they'll follow us blindly into this fight."

"And they shouldn't have to," Lucien said. "This is our business. This is our fight."

We all nodded in agreement.

For the first time since we had each been born, we were all on the same page.

CHAPTER 24
Jade

I had almost fallen asleep when three quick knocks on my door pulled me awake.

"Who is it?" I asked, sitting up and flinging the covers off my legs.

"It's me. Let me in."

Malachi.

I glanced at myself in the mirror on the wall and brushed my frizzy black hair down with my hands before padding over to the door and flinging it open.

He didn't even wait for my invitation before pushing the door open the rest of the way and shoving himself inside.

"Great," I mumbled. "Come on in." I was wearing a thin nightgown that no-doubt would expose far too much if the sun was out, but the darkness protected me.

It always did.

Malachi didn't even greet me. He began pacing

back and forth in the room, muttering to himself and dragging his hands down his face.

"What's going on?" I asked. "Did something happen?"

"No," he shook his head. "Not yet. But it's about to. Everything's going to change, Jade. Everything."

Panic began to creep into my senses. "What do you mean 'everything's going to change'? What's happening?"

I walked to the side of my bed and sat down, bracing myself on the tall bedpost. Malachi dropped his hands and paced over to me. I could see his face clearly now, his eyes were wild and his breathing was shallow.

I had rarely seen him like this.

"Tell me," I insisted.

My mind instantly spiraled to all the worst places. Was Adeline dead? Did Esther turn on us and run away? Was the King coming back to kill me?

Was it my family? My father? Tessa?

"They're coming," Malachi said. "Tomorrow."

"Who's coming?"

"My father and his soldiers. They're coming here tomorrow."

I stood from the bed and moved closer. "What?" I asked. "Why?"

"They've been invited by Seth to discuss business."

"Why would he invite him? He knows we're here and he knows we're not in the King's favor right now!"

"Because I'm supposed to kill him, Jade. Tomorrow. I have no doubt that Seth wants proof and wants it done on his lands."

I shook my head. "It's a setup. It has to be."

Malachi took a deep breath. "I thought the same thing at first."

"What are we going to do about it? Does everyone know?"

"Yes, the others know. My brothers and I have a plan. As long as Seth stays out of the way, we'll do what needs to be done and we'll get out of here by tomorrow night."

My heart was racing in my chest. I put a hand over it to feel the pounding.

The King of Rewyth will be here tomorrow. And Malachi will kill him.

"You'll become the King of Rewyth, then?" I asked, keeping my voice as soft as possible.

Malachi looked at me, a sea of emotions swarming those deep, beautiful eyes. "Yes. I'll become the King of Rewyth. Once we explain that something went terribly wrong during a business deal to Trithen."

"And they'll believe that?"

Malachi nodded. "My father has a lot of enemies. Not just us. I doubt anyone will have a problem with me becoming the King when they learn the news.

Malachi moved and grabbed me by my arms, forcing me to look at him. "You have to do every single thing I tell you to do, Jade. Everything. Can you do that?"

I nodded. "What do you want me to do?"

"I'll need you to stay here. Nobody will step foot inside this castle, but no matter what happens, you can't leave. I won't be able to focus if I think you might be in danger."

"You really think he believes we're in Fearford right now? What if he has spies that went looking for us?"

"If that were the case, they would be here right now. My father is too hot-headed to not act on information like that. If he thought we were here, we would know. There's no way he has any clue. Besides, I killed the King of Trithen. This is the last place he would expect us to go."

That made sense. The fact that Malachi and Seth were now working together was still a strange concept to me. Malachi's father would never expect that.

"Okay," I said. "I'll be hiding out of sight. Where will you be?"

"Killing my father, princess. That's where I'll be."

He had a straight face as he said the words, but I knew they had to hurt. Malachi hated his father. For probably decades, he had been harboring this hatred and hadn't been able to act on it.

He thought his father had been torturing his mother.

How wrong we had all been about that.

"And Esther is okay with this? What does she think about the plan?"

"She'll be okay with it. She hates him even more than the rest of us," he said. "If anything, she'll be angry that she wasn't able to do it herself."

"And your magic... it will keep you safe, right? I mean... isn't this risky?"

Malachi raised an eyebrow. "Worried about me, princess?"

I shrugged out of his grip and walked to the other side of the room. "You know what I mean," I said.

He chuckled once but eventually answered, "We'll be fine. For anyone else, yeah, it would be risky. But with my magic it won't even take more than a minute. Once the King and his men are close by, I'll drop them all with my power, and my brothers will help me finish him off."

I nodded again, taking it all in. The room felt lighter around me, and I suddenly fought the urge to vomit.

"Hey," Malachi said once I placed both my hands on the bedroom wall for support. "Hey, are you okay?"

I felt him come up behind me, close enough to touch me but not quite there.

Was I okay? *Saints, no.* I was far from being okay. Would he understand? He was the one killing his father tomorrow, after all. That had nothing to do with me.

And what was my job? To shut up and stay out of the way?

Malachi set his hands on my back. His warmth behind me was comforting in a way that made my knees weak.

"What happens next?" I asked. "What happens when it's done?"

"We go back to Rewyth," he said. "We go home."

I let a laugh escape me. *Home?* I didn't even know if I had a home anymore. It certainly wasn't here.

Would Rewyth be my home?

Malachi sighed heavily, and his breath on the back of my neck made me shiver. "What do you want?" He asked as if he were reading my thoughts.

What did I want?

My first thought was home. I wanted to go home and be with Tessa.

But did I really? Tessa may not even take me back after everything that happened between Malachi and my father.

That small, crumbling town didn't have anything for me. Did I want to go back there? Back to suffering every single day, selling my soul for a single piece of food?

Esther would likely never let me go back, anyway. If I was the piece to this grand puzzle like she thought I was, I wouldn't be safe there.

Rewyth may have been a prison to me in the past, but it just might be my haven now.

I turned around under Malachi's touch. He was so close, my chest was nearly touching his. "I don't know," I answered honestly. "If I go back home... there's nothing there for me. I'd be waiting to die every single day, just like I was before. But in Rewyth..."

"Rewyth is your home, Jade," he said. His voice was low and serious. "Rewyth will always be a home to you, even if you wish to leave."

I met his gaze. "You would let me leave?"

A sad smile played on his lips. "You're not my prisoner, Jade. My father forced us to marry. When he's dead..."

He didn't have to finish the sentence. I knew what he was thinking.

I shook my head and looked away so Malachi wouldn't see the tears welling up in my eyes. Saints. When had I turned into such a cry baby?

But Malachi grabbed my chin and forced me to look at him.

"You're my wife, Jade. *My wife*. That doesn't change for me. If you wish to go back home and live with your family, I won't stop you. But you are the Princess of Rewyth. If you wish to come with me to rule, I swear I'll make you the happiest woman in the Kingdom."

I couldn't believe he was saying this. My mind raced, running through everything he had said or done to me in the past few weeks.

"Why?" I asked. "I can't keep up, Mal. One second you barely talk to me, the next second you want me to come with you to Rewyth?"

Malachi leaned forward and touched his forehead against mine. My breath hitched.

"I've tried to ignore how I feel about you, Jade. It's safer for everyone if you aren't near me."

"But that's not true. If what Esther is saying is true, there's no place safer for me." He closed his eyes. "I know you didn't expect any of this, either. But I'm involved in all of this, whether we like it or not. I don't think running away is an option for me anymore."

"What are you going to do?"

I couldn't think. Malachi's breath tickled my cheek, invading my thoughts and taking over every emotion. I didn't care about the future. I didn't care. Saints, I never even planned on living this long.

Would it be completely crazy if I went back to Rewyth with Malachi? The Prince of Shadows?

My husband?

"Jade," he whispered, his voice holding the same longing that I was feeling. It wasn't just saying my name. He was begging me.

I pushed myself upward and pressed my lips against his, softly. He froze for a second, but his hands found themselves wrapping around my body, holding me to him.

I kissed Malachi, my husband, like we could forget everything in our crazy, messy lives. Like it was just him and I. His mouth was warm against mine. He kissed me slowly, his hands firm as he held me against him.

I pulled away, just for a second, and looked into his eyes. "I don't know what I want, Mal. I have no damned idea. But I do know that I want you. I want this."

He let out a long breath and said, "Thank the Saints for that, Jade, because I honestly don't know what I would do without you."

And he kissed me back, harder this time. My arms wrapped around his shoulders and he lifted me up against the wall so I could wrap my legs around his waist. Malachi kissed my lips, my neck, my chest. He kissed me until I was drunk on him, drunk on the thought of us together in this frenzy of the night.

His mouth didn't leave mine as he carried me to the massive bed, moving so he was positioned above me on top of the silk sheets.

My heart was pounding in my chest. This was everything that I wanted, everything that I needed. I needed Malachi with me. I had wanted this for longer than I had liked to admit.

Malachi was everything.

His breath was hot on my neck as his mouth moved lower, his hands moving to caress every inch of my body. I arched my back to get closer to him, not wanting a single inch of space between us.

I slid my hands under his loose shirt and up his back, running my fingers across the base of his strong black wings that hovered above us.

Malachi hissed against my neck.

"Careful, princess," he breathed.

Heat rushed to my face, but I didn't stop. I kissed him harshly, pulling his face closer to mine.

"I haven't... I mean I don't know..." I stammered between kisses.

Malachi pulled back, holding himself up above me. A wicked, untethered grin splattered across his face. "Don't worry, princess." He kissed me lightly on the lips. "I want this more than anything, but our first time is not going to be in an enemy kingdom where I am not king," he whispered.

Relief and regret both swarmed my head, and I realized how hard I had been breathing. "Okay," I whispered back, not sure of what else to say.

Malachi didn't move from above me. He brought his hand up to caress my cheek, running his thumb against my skin. "I love you, Jade Weyland. I would burn down any kingdom for you. I hope you know that. After everything, I am yours. I will always be yours."

My chest ached with emotion I didn't know I could ever feel. Yes, we were married. Yes, he had saved my life on more than one occasion.

But hearing those words from him changed everything.

A single tear slipped down my cheek. Malachi quickly wiped it away.

"I love you, too, Malachi."

CHAPTER 25
Malachi

I woke up feeling something I hadn't felt in decades.

Fear.

I wasn't even sure I was capable of fear anymore. Not for my own life, anyway.

Jade still slept next to me. Her features had grown softer since I had known her. She had changed so much since that first day I had seen her hunting in the forest, nearly throwing herself at a pack of wolves to feed her family.

The family that hadn't even wanted her.

Somewhere in the weeks that she had been with us, she had lost a sort of edge that used to consume her. Not in a bad way, no. It was in a way that made me want to protect her with my life.

And I would. I would do anything to protect her.

My father would be dead by the time the sun set. Jade wouldn't be safe until it was done.

And I had decades of pain that screamed for vengeance. Begged for it.

Today would be the day. Today would be the day my father paid for decades of pain. Of torture. Years and years of using me as his own personal weapon.

I had killed mothers. I had killed children. I had slaughtered innocent people time and time again, just because he had commanded it.

Granted, it took me decades to even realize what he was doing. He had been power-hungry as soon as he had learned about my gifts.

"Be careful," he had told me once, the day after we learned of my power. *"People are going to try to exploit this power of yours. They'll try to use it for their own greedy intentions."*

How right he had been.

I didn't feel guilty. I had stopped feeling guilty for the way I felt about my father decades ago.

He deserved to die. His reign had come to an end.

My mind flashed back to the way his guards had thrown Jade to the ground and whipped her right in front of me.

No. I wouldn't have any problem killing my father with my bare hands.

The sun was rising slowly. I marched through the diamond streets of Trithen, making my way to the meeting spot that Seth and I agreed on.

Today would be the day. No mistakes. No errors. No hesitations.

"You're looking rather chipper this morning, brother," Adonis chirped as he swung into step beside me, Lucien following close by.

"Good morning to you, too," I spat. "Where are the twins?"

"We told them to hang back and keep an eye on Adeline, don't worry," he replied. "We execute the plan. We get the Saints out of here. That's it."

"We really think this army of brutes is going to help us with the ambush?" Lucien asked.

"We have to," I said. "And if they turn on us, they'll die."

"You sound confident. That's good," Adonis added. "You better have that same confidence as you push that blade of yours through our father's chest."

"You don't have to worry about me," I said. "Nothing is more important than our father dying today."

They fell into step behind me as we made our way out of the city, toward the front gates.

We didn't see another soul in the morning sun as we made our way to the meeting spot.

A small row of tents became visible at the edge of Trithen's land. A few hundred soldiers sat around, sharpening their weapons and warming up for the day.

My brothers and I ignored them all, walking straight to the largest tent. The tent where Seth would likely be *pretending* to have things under control.

"Seth," I said as I yanked back the flap to the tent. "Is everything in order?"

Seth straightened immediately. He was wearing a

soldier's uniform, a far cry from his usual attire. His right hand rested on the handle of his sword, and his face was dripping in worry.

"Everything is in order," he replied. "Your father and his army should be here within the next couple of hours."

"You're sure about that?" Adonis asked from behind me.

Seth paused for a second before answering. "Are you questioning my intel?"

"Just verifying the facts," Adonis replied. "It's our lives on the line if this goes badly."

"It won't," Seth said. "I'll make sure of that. As long as we all stick to our plan, Malachi here will be the King of Rewyth before lunch is served."

The King of Rewyth.

The words made me stiff. This was the title I was born for. This was the title I had been seeking for decades, waiting for my turn on the throne.

Not for power. Not for popularity. I knew I could be a better leader than my father. I knew I could bring justice to our world in a way that he never had.

Rewyth deserved at least that much.

"Fine," I answered. "I'll find you when it's over." I turned and began exiting the tent, my brothers two paces behind me.

"Don't you want to stay and talk strategy with my advisors?" Seth yelled after me.

"We have a strategy," I yelled back. "And it involves murder, not staring at a useless map. Tell your soldiers to let us handle this, and it'll all be over soon."

Seth didn't follow us as we walked back into the makeshift camp. We recognized most of the soldiers before us, but they didn't speak to us as we walked by.

A few nodded, others looked in the opposite direction, but nobody would be approaching us today.

No, today would be a day of treason.

A day where I killed my own father, the King of Rewyth.

Nobody was going to mess with that.

My brothers and I found a quiet area near the edge of the camp.

"You're sure about this?" Lucien asked. "Feeling up to the task, brother?"

"There's not a doubt in my mind," I replied. It was the truth. I had no hesitation around the fact that killing my father would be as easy as breathing.

"Whatever happens today, brother," he said, "we're on your side. From here on out, we truly are. You haven't been able to trust us in the past, and we understand why. But things are different now. We're on the same team."

Lucien clenched his jaw, but tilted his chin in agreement.

I nodded to Adonis. "Thank you, brother," I replied.

We sat around for another hour, watching the soldiers around us prepare for a war they would have no part in fighting.

Not if everything went according to plan, that is.

Ambush the incoming crew, drop them with my power, and kill my father swiftly. That was the plan, and it was going to work.

It had to work.

My brothers and I didn't fidget. We didn't worry. We showed no signs of nerves. This was not our first war. It wasn't even our fifth war. We had lived through decades fighting battles for our father.

We knew how these things worked. Killing was embedded into our beings.

A horn blared in the distance.

My blood ran cold. I jumped to my feet, hand on my sword, as other soldiers moved into formation around our camp.

My father was nearby.

It was time for a fight.

CHAPTER 26
Malachi

"Get into position!" Seth's voice yelled from behind. Lucien, Adonis and I were already on the move, already rushing in the direction my father's men would be approaching from.

My sword was drawn. My power rumbled with every step I took.

I was power.

I was justice.

And today, I would be executioner.

Seth's men were instructed to stay out of sight unless something went wrong. My brothers and I would handle this on our own. Anyone else involved would be a liability.

My father had no idea that we would be waiting for him. He would be thrown entirely off guard, a perfect opportunity for our attack.

We marched forward, through the thick woods,

until we heard the familiar vibrations of horse footsteps pounding the forest floor below us.

They were here.

"Stay out of sight until I give the signal," I whispered to my brothers. They dispersed on either side of me, following my orders without question.

My blood pumped rapidly through my veins. This was it. This was the moment that would change everything.

I deserved this.

Jade deserved this.

Saints, all of Rewyth deserved this.

The first horse came into view in the narrow path of the forest, the man riding it dodging the large tree branches that hovered. Relief flooded my body. A guard I had worked with dozens of times came fully into view.

"Malachi?" he questioned after he saw me. "Hold up!" he yelled to the party following behind him. My father was close. I could feel it. "What are you doing here? What's going on?"

"I need to speak to my father," I said sharply, loud enough that my father would hear me if he was part of this party.

Show no weakness. Yield no mercy.

"I'm afraid that's not happening right now," the guard responded warily. "Let us pass, and we can discuss whatever business you may have with the King back at Trithen."

He had always been an obedient slave.

They all had been.

But I couldn't blame them. They were just doing whatever it took to survive.

And so was I.

"Thank you, but I think I'll be speaking with my father right now," I said again. His black horse approached me, but I didn't budge. My black wings flared out on either side of me, blocking his path entirely.

The guard unsheathed his sword. "Don't do this, Malachi. Don't start trouble. Let us pass."

Another guard came into view behind him.

"What's going on?" My father's voice boomed from somewhere deeper in the forest.

Every single sense of mine was electrified. This was it. This was the moment I had been waiting on.

"It's your son," the second guard yelled back to my father. "Malachi Weyland."

"What?" My father yelled up. The surprise in his voice told me everything I needed to know. They had no idea we were going to ambush them. The plan was working. "What is he doing here?"

Silence filled the air as the guards waited for me to answer.

"I need to talk to you privately," I yelled.

Commotion from behind the guards told me it was working.

My father was coming forward.

The hair on my neck stood straight up.

"For Saint's sake, Malachi," my father mumbled.

"We don't speak for weeks and you show up here? What do you want?"

He stepped into view, and I was no longer his son. I was a predator stalking his prey.

I felt nothing but numbness mixing with the increasing adrenaline in my blood.

As soon as I could see the sparkle of his wicked blue eyes, I unleashed my power. My brothers were standing behind me, so I aimed the deadly urge at every being before me.

And within a second, I had started a war.

My own power buzzed in my knees. There were six guards, the two in front and four more that had been hiding in the back.

I brought them all down in pain. They slid off their horses and hit the ground, moaning and clutching their chests.

It wouldn't be just pain in their chests, though. Each of their entire bodies would feel like they were nearly exploding by this point.

Including my father, who was on his knees before me, clawing at his own body.

A sight that brought a wicked grin to my face.

"Now, Malachi!" Adonis yelled from behind me.

I brought my sword up and stepped forward. "You have forced me to be a killer many times, father," I said to him, my final words to the man who had brought me so much suffering. "But this time, I choose to be the killer."

And just as I was about to bring the sword down

on my cowering father's head, an arrow ripped through the air from somewhere deeper in the forest.

And pierced me in the shoulder.

I hissed in pain, quickly ripping the long weapon out of my flesh. It wasn't deep and I would heal quickly, but that meant there were more.

We weren't the only ones fighting this fight. The bastard had guards hidden in the forest.

Which meant he had been expecting an ambush.

"Lucien!" I yelled. He moved in an instant to send the signal to the other soldiers that we were in trouble.

Killing my father. That's what I needed to focus on. I didn't care about how many people were shooting at me.

I lifted my sword again, grunting against my pain.

My father looked up at me.

And began to stand.

Along with each of the soldiers.

No, no, no.

I dug deeper to find my power, desperate to belittle them again, to end them all for good.

But there was nothing there.

"Saints," I mumbled to myself. Panic inched its way into my veins.

It had to be that arrow. Laced with something that would block my power from being effective. I had heard stories of herb-laced weapons that would do such things, but I had never seen them myself.

Not until now, anyway.

"What's wrong, son?" my father sneered as he regained traction on his feet. "Plans to kill your own father not going as planned?"

The sarcastic note in his voice made me angrier than ever.

"I don't need magic to kill a bastard. I've done it hundreds of times before, remember?" I sneered.

I swung my sword down, but metal collided with metal.

And that's when absolute chaos erupted.

Seth's soldiers poured in from behind, but my father's men were ready. And they were trained in combat much more extensively than these men were.

"Malachi!" Adonis yelled from my right. "Malachi, watch out!"

A sharp pain sliced through my right arm. I spun around to see a young soldier with a knife impaled in my skin.

I cut him down quickly with my sword, no hesitation.

No hesitation in war. Hesitating meant dying.

I was not dying today.

I turned back to where my father was, and he simply stood with a nasty grin on his face.

"You're dead," I sneered. The words came out in a low growl.

Did he not believe me? Did he truly believe he could get out of this? He was outnumbered by hundreds.

One of Seth's men sliced his weapon through the one guard that had remained by my father.

And then there was a clear path to him.

There was nobody left to defend him. Nobody left to help him. Yet he was still the same, arrogant bastard that he always was.

He did not reach for his weapon. He did not try to run.

I took three steps between us and grabbed my father by the throat. "You deserve a worse death than this one," I sneered.

"Is that what your mother told you?" he managed to get out.

"Don't talk about her."

He laughed wickedly. "I knew she had something to do with this. Trust me, son. You don't want to listen to a word she says. There's a reason she left Rewyth."

"I'm well aware of the fact that she left you and your wicked ways," I said. "It's something I should have done long ago."

"She'll say anything to use your power," my father continued. His voice had changed from confident to desperate. "Believe me, son. Believe me! Was this her idea? This ambush?"

My blood was pounding in my ears. Yells of pain rang out around me, each of my fathers men dying.

Even the ones that had been hiding away in the trees. The ones with arrows.

They were all going to die. They were no match for an army.

And my father was no match for me.

"No," I said. "Killing you was my idea."

I let go of his throat and drew my sword.

Blood rushing through my veins hissed in my ears. The grip on my weapon was tight. I did not shake. I did not falter. This was something that had to be done. I had no doubt in my mind.

I was a killer. I had killed hundreds of people who didn't deserve it.

This was not going to be one of those times.

With the exhale of a breath, I brought the sword down. It crashed through my father's body with ease.

And his dead body fell to the ground with a thud.

I breathed in.

I breathed out.

It was over. I had done it.

"Malachi!" Serefin's voice pulled me from my trance.

There was still fighting going on around me.

"Enough!" Seth's voice boomed louder than mine, halting the fighting where it stood. "Surrender or die," he said to the rest of my father's men. "This fight is over."

The men dropped to their knees in surrender.

My breath became heavier and heavier.

I had just killed my father.

"Mal," Serefin said again, softer this time. I looked for him in the crowd of soldiers, and when my eyes finally landed on him, my stomach sank.

"Eli?" Lucien yelled, stepping forward.

No, no, no.

My feet moved without my permission, bringing me closer to where Eli knelt over another soldier.

No, not just another soldier.

His twin brother, Fynn.

Eli's head was now bowed, his body shaking in silent sobs.

"Fynn?" Adonis asked. All three of us now stood around them both.

"He was protecting me," Eli said after a few moments, his voice barely audible. "We came here to help, but everyone was already fighting when we got here. He tried...he tried–"

Adonis dropped to his knees beside Eli, checking Fynn's pulse. Blood smeared his neck, his chest. Too much blood.

When he couldn't find a pulse, he bowed his head in defeat.

It confirmed what the dread in the air was telling me. Fynn, our brother, was dead.

Lucien cursed beneath his breath. "You should have stayed out of this," he mumbled to Eli. Adonis shot him a warning glance, but Lucien didn't stop. "You two should have stayed behind like you were supposed to!"

Eli looked up at us and yelled, "Isaiah told us you needed help! He said you asked for us to come fight with you!"

Rage blurred my vision. *This was a set up.*

Seth approached me in the crowd, his soldiers parting way to make room.

"Well done, Malachi," he smiled. "I knew you would be able to complete the task. No motivation is stronger than revenge, right?" he asked.

Something in his voice was off, though.

And something in his eyes had changed.

I knew that look. I had seen it before.

Betrayal.

"How does it feel?" Seth asked. "Killing your own father? I planned on doing it myself, truly, just to show you what it felt like to have your own family murdered. But, well, it was so much easier having you do it yourself."

No. This couldn't be happening.

I lifted my sword again, holding it between Seth and myself.

"What did you do?" I asked Seth.

A few guards stepped forward to protect Seth. My brothers held up their own weapons.

"You sick bastard," Lucien sneered from beside me. "We were working with you as a courtesy. You did this. You killed Fynn!" He stepped forward again, sword raised.

"I wouldn't do that if I were you," Seth replied calmly.

"Yeah?" I responded. "Why not?"

"If anything happens to me, your brothers won't be the only one that gets hurt. Your precious bride will die, too."

My heart skipped a beat. "You're lying."

"Am I?" he asked. "Or is our friend Isaiah keeping

her company right now, waiting to kill her at the very command?"

CHAPTER 27

Jade

Pounding on my door jolted me from my deep sleep, some of the only restful sleep I had gotten in weeks.

"What do you want?" I yelled at the door, scrambling out of bed and looking around for Malachi.

Who was nowhere to be seen.

"Jade, it's me," Isaiah said. "I need to talk to you."

"Right now?" I asked. I didn't try to hide the annoyance in my voice. I wrapped my arms around my body, hugging my thin nightgown, as I stomped to the door and cracked it open. "What could possibly be so important, Isaiah?"

"Can I come in?"

"Seriously?"

He didn't answer me, just stood there expectantly.

With a sigh, I let him in.

And instantly felt a shift in energy. "What's going on?" I asked. Isaiah paced back and forth in the room, not making eye contact with me. He even moved to bite the nails on one hand. In the days that I had known Isaiah, he struck me as a confident guy. Even too confident, at times.

This was a side of him I had never seen. "Isaiah," I said, approaching him slowly. "I need you to tell me what's wrong. Is it the King?"

He stopped pacing and faced me. "Get dressed," he said. His voice shook.

"For what?"

"Just get dressed, and I'll tell you when we're on the way."

I crossed my arms. "I'm not doing anything until you tell me why you're acting crazy."

"Fine," he spat. "You want to know why I'm freaking out? The King of Rewyth is on his way here right now and your husband is going to kill him. We're in a kingdom full of people who hate humans, and we're about to be in the middle of a war."

"You're being dramatic," I said. "Malachi will kill the King and this entire thing will be over."

"Seriously?" he said. "You're really that naive?"

I had considered the idea that something might go wrong today, but at the end of the day, Malachi was the most powerful fae in both of these kingdoms. Nobody would hurt him. The King didn't stand a chance, especially since he lost his one bargaining chip.

Me.

"Look, Jade," he said. "I know you're married to Malachi. I know you're loyal to that agreement, whatever that means. But we can get out of here right now, you and me. Say the word, and we'll go."

His eyes were frantically scanning me, searching for any inkling of hesitation. "I-" I stuttered. "I can't, Isaiah. I'm sorry, really. I know my life in the human world would be easier but I just can't leave everyone. Not after everything we've been through."

Isaiah took a deep, uneven breath. "Fine," he said. "I tried, Jade. I really did. I tried to warn you about the fae, I tried to offer you something better. But at the end of the day, you really love him, don't you?"

I shrugged. "What do you want me to say? He's my husband now, Isaiah. He'll always protect me. Always."

"We're counting on it," he said. Something in his face changed, darkened, and he turned his attention to my bedroom door. "Guards!" he yelled.

Two soldiers stormed into the room, coming straight for me.

"What the Saints is this?" I yelled at him. "What are you doing?"

The guards grabbed me by each of my arms, not giving me time to react.

"I'm sorry, Jade," Isaiah said. "It has to be this way."

One of the guards forced a small cloth over my nose and mouth, and the smell of something foul ripped through my lungs.

I wanted to scream. Malachi. Malachi would help me.

But before I could even yell, my world went black.

CHAPTER 28

Malachi

"Where is she?" I demanded. "If you even thought about touching her, you won't walk out of here alive."

Seth laughed, his white teeth gleaming off his blood-stained face. "And you think I'm just going to tell you?" he spat.

I was going to kill him. I was going to burn his entire damned kingdom to the ground and take everything for myself.

Seth had turned out to be a manipulative, sneaky bastard.

"Tell me where she is," I said carefully, "and you have a chance of getting out of here alive."

"Fine," he said after eyeing me. "But she'll be dead before you get to her."

But I had no choice. I would do anything for her. I would burn any kingdom to the ground if it meant she was safe.

Seth's guards approached, and I fought every instinct to slaughter each one of them.

"Happy now?" I questioned. "Happy that you can control me?"

"Yes," he answered quickly. "Very happy. Now you have two options. You can stay here and kill us all, or go save your wife. Which do you choose?"

He pointed to the large field.

"Serefin, stay here with Eli!" I yelled before taking off in a full sprint.

I didn't glance back at my brothers, but I knew they would be following my every move.

They had followed me to battle, they had helped me slaughter our father. We had all been betrayed, but for once in my life I was certain they were just as blind as I was.

I would kill Isaiah for this. If one of them didn't beat me to it.

I ran in the direction that Seth had indicated, stepping over the dozens of bodies that littered the field.

It wasn't my first time in a battle, if that's what you would even call this. It certainly wouldn't be my last.

Death was a weakness. Being sensitive to death was a weakness.

"None of you will survive this," I whispered to myself. "None of you."

My power was nearly recovered, I was seconds away from releasing it on anyone who dared to cross me, when Jade's voice entered the clearing.

"Someone get me out!" she screamed. I was certain the others couldn't hear it.

Only me. Because it was just for me.

"Where is she!" I yelled. My voice shook, I didn't care. I needed her. I needed her back. "I'm coming, Jade!" I yelled. I thought I heard her voice yell something back, but I couldn't be sure, I couldn't be certain that it was her.

My blood was pumping through my ears, Saints. I couldn't think clearly. Couldn't act clearly. One foot after another, one foot after another I ran to her.

"I'm coming, Jade!" I yelled again. "Just hang on, I'm coming!"

Seth's laughter in the distance was the only thing I heard as I turned the corner around the wall.

And saw Jade.

Trapped in a massive cage made of what appeared to be...*bones.*

"Jade," I breathed. "Jade, are you alright?"

I closed the distance between us in seconds. "Are you alright?" I repeated.

Although she was clearly not alright. Blood smeared the bones that held her inside, and tears streamed down her face, dripping from her chin.

"Jade," I mumbled.

"I'm fine, Malachi," she insisted. "I'm fine, but you're in danger. Isaiah, he set me up. This was all a trap, you have to run Mal. You have to run!"

Part of me, the primal part, wanted me to run for the hills. To ditch this place and never come back.

But the other part of me wanted to rip apart anyone who thought they could take Jade from me.

Perhaps that part of me was even more primal. These bastards touched my wife and they thought they could live.

It was certainly not an option.

But we would have to move fast.

Inside the cage, unconscious and lying on the ground, was a deadling.

CHAPTER 29
Jade

We were alone, but not for long. Commotion behind Malachi told me that others would be coming soon.

Every inch of my body stung with pain.

"We have to get you out of here," Malachi growled, pulling on the bones that held me inside. He was covered with blood, it dripped freely from his arm.

Something had gone terribly wrong.

"I already tried that," I yelled. "It won't budge!"

The deadling beside me began to twitch.

It was going to wake up and kill me.

I took a deep, shaking breath and tried to think.

Was this Seth's plan all along? To have Malachi watch me get ripped to shreds while Seth sat there and watched? Was this his sick form of revenge?

"Do something!" I screamed.

"Jade," Malachi said. "Jade, I need you to listen to me. I need you to use your magic."

"What?"

"Your magic, Jade! We don't have a choice!"

"No, no! I can't!"

"That thing will wake up, and then it will kill you, Jade. Do you understand? You will *die* if you do not use your magic to break out of this damned cage. You have to do it!"

"I..."

"You have to!"

The creature, just feet away from me, began to move more and more. A sickening growl escaped its jaws.

Saints. It was waking up.

I tried to control my breathing. I tried to dig deep into that grounding energy that Esther had tried to teach me, but all I found was panic.

I was panicking.

Malachi had no choice but to watch in horror.

The creature grunted and growled as it fully awoke, moving to stand on its feet.

And then it realized I was in there with him. Its black eyes locked on me.

"No," I whispered to myself. "No, I'm not dying this way."

"Dig deep, Jade," Malachi whispered in desperation between the cage bars next to me. "Dig deep, and you'll find what you need."

I squeezed my eyes shut and reopened them.

The ugly creature began moving toward me.

"I can't do it," I whispered.

"Yes, you can," he repeated. His voice held an emotion I had never heard before, an emotion that made me want to try.

Made me want to *live*.

Snapping jaws came closer and closer.

Breathe, Jade. Focus.

I was the peacemaker.

The key to the prophecy.

I was going to survive this.

I closed my eyes one last time, feeling warmth from Malachi's body behind me through the cage bars.

I felt the smallest inkling of power light up in my stomach. It was small, but I pulled on it, on the small fire that began lighting up inside of me.

I pulled and pulled and pulled.

Desperation kicked in, I would do *anything* to make this work. I would do *anything* to save myself.

"Saints, save us," Malachi whispered behind me.

Heat overtook me.

And everything erupted at once.

CHAPTER 30
Malachi

Every bone in my body ached as I scrambled to my feet, desperate to find Jade. The bone cage that had encapsulated her just seconds ago was now ash.

And the deadling had disintegrated with it.

"Holy Saints," I mumbled, taking in the scene around me. "Jade, are you okay?"

She sat on her knees, hugging herself around her waist. I ran to her side. "Jade, answer me. Are you okay?"

"Yes," she mumbled. My chest dropped to my stomach. "Yes, I'm okay."

Adonis and Lucien jogged up to the scene. "What happened?" they asked.

"Where's everyone else?" I asked.

"Eli won't leave Fynn. Serefin is protecting him. The other bastards already left, though."

"Is Seth dead?" I asked. "Please tell me one of you killed him."

My brothers looked at each other before looking back at me. "Not yet," Adonis answered.

"What are you still standing here for?" I asked. "Adonis, go find him and rip his head off. Lucien, I need you to bring Isaiah to me. I want to kill that traitor bastard myself."

Again, they didn't move.

"Are you two deaf?"

"We can't, brother."

"What do you mean you can't?"

Esther appeared out of nowhere, as if she had been there all along. "They mean they can't, son. Because I ordered them not to. I need Seth and Isaiah alive."

I stood, Jade rising slowly with me. "Excuse me?"

"I told them not to kill Seth and Isaiah, and they have no choice but to obey me."

If I had my power back, she would be on her knees.

They all would.

"And why would you do something like that?" I asked. "They betrayed me. They betrayed us, and they nearly killed Jade."

"I swear to you, Malachi, I didn't know they were going to hurt Jade. I didn't know they were going to threaten your brothers. Seth's past vendetta with you ran deeper than I had anticipated."

"You've been working with Seth, protecting him behind my back? For what? What is he doing for you?"

She didn't answer me. Didn't blink.

"Adonis? Lucien?"

More silence.

Esther, my mother, looked at them and nodded. Just once.

"We're sorry, brother," Adonis said, stepping forward. "I don't want to do this. You know I have no choice."

"Do what," I said as he took another step. Lucien followed. "Adonis, what are you doing?"

When I looked at Esther again, she looked down to her feet. "It's more complicated than us," she said. "This is more than just you and me, son. Sacrifices must be made. It will all be worth it in the end. Jade is the peacemaker, and we'll need her to do many things for us to fulfill the prophecy. She'll be the key to give the witches our power back. We'll be able to use our magic again without sacrifices. We'll be just as powerful as the fae once this is all over, son. But we can't have you getting in the way. I hope you understand."

"If I could stop it, I would," Lucien said. "We can't control it." Lucien unsheathed the blade at his hip.

They were going to kill me.

Under Esther's control, they would have no choice but to do it.

"No," I said, it came out in a whisper. I took a step back, Jade moving with me as she clung to my back. "Don't."

Adonis's brows furrowed, the only sign of regret. Of grief.

"Esther, stop this right now!"

283

She looked away.

"It's already been done, son."

My brothers both took another step forward.

"He told me not to trust you. His dying words to me were to stay away from you," I breathed to Esther.

No. Things weren't going to end like this. Not after everything. I had sacrificed too much. I had waited too long.

My heartbeat screamed at me to do something.

I couldn't think. I could only act.

There was one person here Esther would never risk losing.

With a roar of frustration, I stepped back once more and gripped Jade's arm, flinging her to the front of my body as she let out a scream.

"Trust me," I whispered to her. She would understand. She had to. She was a survivor, just like me.

I unsheathed my own knife, the small one I had kept at my hip. My brothers stopped where they stood.

Jade was frozen before me as I held her body to mine, confused and disoriented and barely there.

My hands shook for the first time all day.

I looked at Esther, my mother, who I believed was on my side this entire time.

"You kill me, your precious peacemaker dies, too."

And I pressed the blade to Jade's throat.

CHAPTER 31
Jade

I t wasn't real. It wasn't real. It wasn't real.

That's what I was telling myself.

But the blade to my throat was *very* real.

And the man holding me tightly to his chest was just as real.

I didn't move. Didn't blink. My breath came out in shallow pants as I tried to decipher Mal's next move.

"You won't," Esther whispered, but her eyes were wider than I had ever seen them.

"I will," Malachi growled. The vibrations of his feral voice rumbled through my weak body.

If Malachi hadn't been holding me up, I would have been right back on the ground.

"You swore to protect her," Esther spat. "She is your *wife*. Jade is not a martyr, she is the peacemaker! She is the key to everything! She is the key to equality within our realm!"

Malachi shook me harshly. "I know what she is!" he

yelled. I flinched with every word. "I will be protecting her from the plan you have to use her for your own good!"

Esther stepped forward, hands in front of her. Wild eyes landed on me, then back to Malachi who still held me tightly.

"Don't take another step," Malachi warned. He pressed the blade into my skin, just under my chin, until I felt the sharp sting.

No.

He was really cutting me.

"End the blood oath with my brothers, and everyone here can live. It doesn't have to be this way," Malachi said. I could hear his effort to regain control of his emotions, but the *sane* Malachi was gone. The Prince of Shadows stood in his place.

"You think I believe you won't kill me the second I free them?" Esther questioned.

Adonis and Lucien stood in limbo, half-ready to obey Esther's orders. Half-ready to end Malachi's life.

But also half-ready to kill Esther where she stood.

"Why?" I managed to say, although my voice came out as a low squeak. Malachi instantly stiffened behind me. "You helped us," I pleaded to Esther. "He's your son, and we were in this together. We were working together."

"Your husband is right," she replied reluctantly. "The prophecy requires more than I had let on before."

"Like what, specifically?" Malachi asked.

"When our power is returned to the witches, the peacemaker must fulfill one last piece."

"Which is?" Malachi pushed.

My stomach dropped as the realization of the situation washed over me. "I'll end up dead, anyway. And the witches will have control of all magic."

Malachi's grip on me tightened, and the blade he had barely loosened on my neck was sharp against me once again.

I yelped at the sting of pain.

"Is that true?" Malachi asked.

Esther's silence was the answer. She never expected me to live. I was merely here to fulfill her prophecy.

"Break it. Now," he demanded. "Break the blood oath."

Esther hesitated. "You need me alive," she said. "If you kill me right now, Jade is as good as dead."

"Isn't she already, anyway?" he asked.

"No," Esther replied. "There's another way. I swear it. But you'll need my help. I'm the only one who knows all the details on breaking the prophecy. Word has gotten out now, they'll be coming for her. You know they will."

"Who?"

"The witches of the Paragon. They'll come for her so they can control the magic."

An eerie silence stilled the air around us.

"Fine," Malachi spat after a few moments. "End the blood oath with my brothers, and you can live."

"You swear it?" Esther asked.

"By the Saints who dwell within us."

Esther stepped in front of Lucien and Adonis and chanted something quietly that I couldn't make out. The brothers glanced at each other once before they snapped, both physically being pushed away from Esther by a force we could not see.

"They're free," Esther said after the invisible force stopped. Malachi released a breath against my ear.

And all at once, as quickly as it had begun, it was over.

Malachi released his deadly grip on me, and I sank to my knees before him.

A sob shook my body.

What had just happened?

I was covered in blood now, some mine, some Malachi's.

My hands shook as I held them out in front of me.

"Jade," Malachi whispered as he knelt next to me. He reached a hand out gently.

"No! Don't–" I said, scrambling away from him on the ground. Who was this man? This wasn't the Prince of Shadows who would do anything to protect me, no. This was a stranger. A stranger who had *hurt* me.

My fingers moved to the cut on my throat, feeling the wet blood.

"Okay," he said, holding his hands up in surrender. "Jade, I'm sorry," he pleaded. His voice cracked as he crumbled entirely next to me. "I'm sorry, Jade. I was desperate, I had no other way out. They were going to kill us both! I would never hurt you, I wouldn't–"

"Stop," I breathed. "Stay away from me. I don't want you to touch me right now. I don't want any of this. I just want to go home."

Malachi's eyes were frantic, searching my face for any sign of forgiveness.

But I had none. I had nothing left to give.

A familiar numbness spread through my chest.

"I won't let them hurt you," Malachi whispered to me. The tears that streamed down his face matched the tears of my own.

They were tears of defeat. Tears of betrayal.

But it was too late. It didn't matter what Malachi said about protecting me. I knew he would, I knew he would lay down his own life for me. But at what cost? When did it end?

My entire body collapsed on the ground as voices around me blurred together.

Malachi wasn't going to let anyone else have me.

Dead or alive.

CHAPTER 32
Jade

"Good," Adeline's soft voice pierced the black pit of my consciousness. "You're awake. Jade, can you hear me?"

I blinked my eyes open, finding myself in a bedroom that looked familiar. "Adeline?" I asked.

"It's me," she replied. Her warm hands rubbed my stiff arm. "You're safe, Jade. You're home."

I lifted my head, but sharp pain shot through my head. *Home? Where was home?* "Where is everyone?" I managed to ask through the dryness in my throat.

"Malachi is safe. He's here. Everyone else is here, too. Esther, Isaiah, Sadie, Eli. They're all here. My brother is keeping the traitors in...*fair* conditions. He's just been worried about you, Jade. That's all."

I hated that I felt relief.

"He almost killed me," I croaked, recalling the events I could remember. I had never heard Malachi so...*monstrous*.

A chill ran down my spine just thinking about it.

"Look, Jade," Adeline said, lowering her voice. "A lot of things happened back in Trithen." She turned her gaze toward the ceiling and blinked back tears. "My brother died. Eli can barely get out of bed. Adonis and Lucien are going crazy thinking about avenging Fynn's death. And Malachi..."

"I don't want to hear about him," I interrupted. "I don't care."

Adeline grabbed each of my arms. "You say that, Jade, but you don't understand. You don't understand what he would do to protect you."

I sat up slightly in bed. "I do know. I know that he's the Prince of Shadows. He's deadly and dangerous and vengeful. And just when I thought he would do anything to protect me...just when I thought I could actually trust a fae...*he's* the one with a blade to my throat. *He's* the one who threatened my life."

Adeline bowed her head and took a deep breath. I knew she understood me. I knew she had her own life controlled by men before, she would understand this.

But Malachi was still her brother.

Tears stung my eyes as I looked at my friend. Adeline was beautiful and strong and compassionate. Yet she still wanted Malachi and I to be together.

"I thought I loved him," I started to say before my voice cracked. Adeline knew what I was trying to say, though. She always knew. "I thought I loved him, Adeline, and he turned on me."

She looked at me with fierce eyes. "He didn't,

though. He didn't give up on you, Jade. Look, I've never seen my brother act this way. He's...he's a completely different person. He can barely live with himself for what he did to you. Just don't give up on him so quickly, okay? There's someone in there worth saving."

I let the tears fall from my eyes.

I had given Malachi a chance already. I wasn't sure how many more I had left to give him.

CHAPTER 33
Malachi

I straightened my tunic and leaned back at the large dining room table.

My palms were sweaty as I rubbed them together. She should be here by now. She should have been here ten minutes ago. Saints, why was I nervous?

I glanced around the room one more time, making sure everything was perfect.

It *had* to be perfect. This might be my only chance I had at talking to Jade, at convincing her to forgive me.

She had needed space over the last few days, I understood that. I needed space, too, after everything that happened.

I also knew that if I even laid eyes on her while her neck wound was still healing, the wound that *I* had inflicted, I would have nothing left to live for.

I screwed up. I was willing to admit that. But she had to understand that I was doing what was best for us. I would protect her to any end, but I couldn't do that if I was dead. I couldn't let my brothers kill me.

The service door to the room creaked open. "She's here, Sir," one of the servants announced.

"Great," I replied, sitting up in my chair. "Send her in."

The air in the room buzzed with electricity as Jade entered.

Her black, silky hair was flowing freely around her shoulders. She wore a long, black dress that swooshed at her ankles as she walked forward and sat down at the end of the massive table, as far as possible from me.

I nodded a greeting. Jade didn't so much as look at me.

"Thank you for joining me," I said. "I know this probably isn't what you expected."

Still, nothing. I blinked once. Twice.

"And I'm sure you have a lot of questions about the future, about *your* future here in Rewyth."

"I want to go home," Jade said. It was the first thing she had said to me in days. Her voice was different. It was...empty.

"You can't," I said coldly. "You'll die there."

Her nostrils flaring was the only hint of a reaction.

"What about my family?" she asked. "What if they're already dead? What if the Paragon already came for them?"

I took a deep, calming breath. I knew she would come with these questions. And I knew how to answer them.

"We'll send someone for your family. We'll bring them here. They'll be safe, just like you."

"And the Paragon? They'll allow that?"

I took another deep breath and looked Jade in the eyes. "I didn't want to tell you this, Jade, but you need to prepare yourself. The Paragon knows you're the peacemaker. They'll use you to break the curse. You're being hunted every day, and others are coming for you."

She didn't respond for a long while. "I've been used as a tool many times before, as you know very well by now. This won't be the first time. I'm sure it won't even be the last."

Emotion I couldn't even explain rushed through my body. I clenched my jaw, desperate not to show it. Not to Jade. Not now.

"Do you think I liked hurting you, Jade?" I asked. I couldn't stop my voice from cracking. "Do you think I *liked* holding a blade to your throat? I did that so we could *live*, Jade."

"I was wrong to think you would protect me," Jade answered. "You're fae. You're selfish. You'll do whatever it takes to survive."

A growl escaped me. I *needed* her to understand.

"They can't have you, Jade. I'm not letting them take you and use you like some weapon. I'm *protecting* you, just like I always have been."

Jade stared at me, jaw clenched.

"Then what do we do?" she asked eventually. "You bring my family here and keep me locked up? You're the King of Rewyth now, so tell me. What are we going to do, Malachi?"

I took a deep, shaking breath. "If the price of winning is Paragon blood being shed, *princess,* then Paragon blood will be shed." I stated. "We will go to war against the Paragon."

Also by Emily Blackwood

CPSIA information can be obtained
at www.ICGtesting.com
Printed in the USA
LVHW111144301122
734324LV00005B/308